A MAN LIKE O'ROURKE

A MAN LIKE O'ROURKE

Jeanne Whitmee

Chivers Press • G.K. Hall & Co.
Bath, England Thorndike, Maine USA

This Large Print edition is published by Chivers Press, England, and by G.K. Hall & Co., USA.

Published in 1999 in the U.K. by arrangement with the author, care of Dorian Literary Agency.

Published in 1999 in the U.S. by arrangement with Dorian Literary Agency.

U.K. Hardcover ISBN 0-7540-3842-4 (Chivers Large Print)
U.K. Softcover ISBN 0-7540-3843-2 (Camden Large Print)
U.S. Softcover ISBN 0-7838-8654-3 (Nightingale Series Edition)

Copyright © Jeanne Whitmee 1987

All rights reserved.

The text of this Large Print edition is unabridged.
Other aspects of the book may vary from the original edition.

Set in 16 pt. New Times Roman.

Printed in Great Britain on acid-free paper.

British Library Cataloguing in Publication Data available

Library of Congress Cataloging-in-Publication Data

Whitmee, Jeanne.
    A man like O'Rourke / by Jeanne Whitmee.
       p.   cm.
    ISBN 0-7838-8654-3 (lg. print : sc : alk. paper)
    1. Large type books.   I. Title.
    [PR6073.H65M36   1999]
    823'.914—dc21   99–15671

LINCOLNSHIRE
COUNTY COUNCIL

CHAPTER ONE

'By the way, Cara. You'll be working with a different photographer on this feature.' Anita French, editor of 'Zena' magazine, looked up from her desk as Cara finished making notes. 'Janet Lorimar's publishers have insisted on using Corin O'Rourke. It seems he's done a lot of their publicity pictures in the past and they have some sort of contract with him.' She smiled. 'I suppose we're lucky really. He's in great demand.'

Cara closed the folder and put it away in her briefcase before looking up at her editor without enthusiasm. 'I hope you're right.'

Anita took off her spectacles and looked at her young features editor, her eyebrows rising slightly. 'You sound a little less than delighted unless I'm very much mistaken!'

Cara shrugged. 'It's just that I've heard he's difficult to work with, that's all.'

Anita slipped her glasses back into place, looking relieved. 'As long as that's all. I'm sure you can handle him. He is the best freelance photographer in the business.' She looked up at Cara. 'For a moment I was afraid he might be an ex-boyfriend or something. We can do without that kind of complication!'

'No fear of that!' Cara snorted. 'By all accounts, the man's the worst kind of chauvinist. I suppose it comes from working with models who haven't a thought in their heads beyond their appearance!'

Anita looked at Cara speculatively. She had worked on 'Zena' magazine since leaving college two years ago and had risen from typist to the position of features editor in record time. She was career minded and ambitious and she worked hard and imaginatively; Anita had no complaints to make on that score. There was just this slight prejudice as far as men were concerned. She had noticed that it sometimes got in the way of her working relationships. She decided that they knew one another well enough now for her to broach the subject. Taking her glasses off again she leaned towards Cara confidentially.

'I've been meaning to have a word with you ...' The telephone on her desk shrilled impatiently and she drew in a sharp, irritated breath. 'Damn!' She picked up the receiver and spoke into it: 'Hang on for just a minute, will you!' She put a hand over the mouthpiece and said to Cara: 'Look—are you free for lunch? I'd like to talk to you.'

Cara nodded and got to her feet, gathering up her things. 'Fine. Round the corner at Mario's—around one?'

The editor nodded. 'Pick me up here. I'll try to be ready.'

Back in her own office Cara opened her folder. She was quite excited about the feature on best-selling novelist Janet Lorimar, and looking forward to interviewing her. The novelist was notoriously reclusive and it was quite a scoop to have managed to persuade her into being the subject of a spread in 'Zena'. It was to coincide with the publication of her latest book and Cara had promised to work in close cooperation with the publishers. Janet's editor had insisted on being present at the interview and photographic sessions which were to take place tomorrow; that had been one of the conditions they had made and Cara had promised to keep to it.

The whole of tomorrow had been left clear so that she would have plenty of time to give to Janet's interview and Cara intended to spend this morning working out the questions she would ask so as to get the very best out of it. She had spent the past week gathering information about the novelist's background; her education in Scotland, her two husbands, one of whom was a T.V. director—her early career as an actress. She opened her folder in anticipation and had just started work when the telephone rang. She picked up the receiver with a sigh.

'Hello, Cara Dean speaking.'

'Good morning.' The caller had a deep male voice with the faintest hint of an Irish accent. She didn't recognise it.

'Hello there. I don't think we've met before, Cara. O'Rourke is the name—Corin

3

O'Rourke.'

Cara was not impressed by the bonhomie. 'Good morning, Mr O'Rourke. Is there something I can do for you?' She placed a slight emphasis on the word 'Mr'. Obviously the man thought he was going to be able to have things all his own way just by turning on the charm. Well, he was about to learn differently!

There was a low chuckle at the other end of the line. 'Oh, I'm *sure* there is. You sound like a very cooperative lady to me. It's just that my work schedule is rather overbooked tomorrow, so I wondered if you'd rearrange things so that we can do the Janet Lorimar session this morning. I can meet you there in about half an hour if that's okay with you?'

Cara felt her scalp prickle with annoyance. 'It *isn't* as a matter of fact,' she told him icily. 'For all sorts of reasons. It's all arranged for tomorrow. Miss Lorimar may not be free, anyway.'

'Oh she is, as a matter of fact. I rang her to ask—and she's quite willing if you are. In fact it's all laid on. All you have to do is turn up.'

Cara almost exploded with anger. 'I see! I'm beginning to wonder why you even bothered to ring me!' she told him.

'Ah now, don't be like that.' The voice was smooth and velvety. 'I only meant to save you trouble. It's just the photographs I want to do. You can still go there and do your interview

4

tomorrow.'

Really! The nerve of the man! 'Can I? *Thanks!*'

'As a matter of fact you needn't come at all if you've too much to do,' he told her coolly. 'I've photographed Miss Lorimar a good many times before, so she'll be quite relaxed with me.'

Cara bristled, thinking of the carefully prepared list of pictures she had planned for her layout. 'Half an hour, I think you said. I'll be there, Mr O'Rourke.' And she slammed the receiver down before she could hear his amused chuckle at the other end of the line.

Janet Lorimar lived in a beautiful and fashionable apartment overlooking Regent's Park. Cara didn't know in what part of London O'Rourke had his studio, but she hoped to be there before him. She walked out of the office into Covent Garden and made her way towards the underground station, then she changed her mind. It looked like rain. Just this once she would treat herself to a taxi. She turned and made her way down towards The Strand, but every taxi that came along seemed to be occupied. The expected April shower began in earnest and she was almost down as far as Charing Cross before she saw one with its light on. Stepping forward, she held up her hand, but a man waving a rolled umbrella got there before her. A bus sped past splashing through a puddle and before she could jump out of the way her skirt was soaked with dirty water. She gave up and bolted down the nearest underground entrance, dabbing at her skirt with a handful of tissues as she went. It was going to be one of those days, she reflected wryly. Once the day's routine was thrown out everything seemed to go wrong. It was always the same. She cursed the cavalier O'Rourke under her breath, making up her mind before they met that he was going to be the kind of man she loathed.

When she arrived at the entrance to the apartment block Cara noticed a rather conspicuous car standing outside. It was a vintage Bentley, large and dark green, its bonnet sporting a broad leather strap. The number plate read: COR 1 and through the window she could see various bits of photographic equipment lying on the passenger seat. It could only belong to one person. O'Rourke had beaten her to it after all!

The door to the apartment was opened by a plump, middle-aged woman who showed Cara through to a sunny room overlooking the park. Wide glass doors were open and led out onto a paved, glass-covered patio edged with flower-filled pots. Janet Lorimar, dressed in a floating pink chiffon evening dress, was reclining on a sun lounger, her back to Cara, while a tall man with a shock of chestnut hair and a luxuriant beard to match squatted on a low wall, firing

6

away at her with his camera. Cara stood watching from the doorway while the camera clicked and whirred, the man encouraging his subject flattering—cajoling—smiling:

'Give me that enigmatic little smile—fine! Now the head back a little—turn and look over your shoulder at me—*beautiful* . . .'

Cara cleared her throat and stepped forward. 'I'm sorry I'm late. I couldn't get a taxi.'

Janet Lorimar looked round. 'Miss Dean! You've arrived.' She looked at Cara's damp skirt. 'Oh dear, did you get caught in the shower? If you'd rung I'd have sent my car for you.' She stood up. 'Actually there was no need for you to come at all. Corin has been managing beautifully.'

Cara bit back a retort. 'There are some shots I particularly want him to get. I'd already planned what I wanted for the feature, you see. He wouldn't have known . . .' She glanced towards the bearded giant still seated on the wall, his arms folded. Obviously he hadn't thought her worth standing up for. He was appraising her lazily with insolent blue eyes, raking her from head to foot. She felt her cheeks colour. What was it about his expression that made her feel as though her clothes had suddenly become transparent? Her hand went to her damp, untidy hair in an involuntary gesture as she said:

'Mr O'Rourke and I haven't actually met—

except on the telephone.'

Janet Lorimar laughed. 'Really? Then come and be introduced. Funny, I took it for granted you'd know each other, being in the same business as it were.'

Taking Cara's hand she drew her out onto the patio. 'Corin, meet the lady you're going to be working with. Cara Dean of "Zena" magazine.'

O'Rourke uncoiled his long length. He must have been well over six feet tall with broad, powerful-looking shoulders. He wore jeans and a white cotton shirt, open at the neck to reveal the thick dark hair that curled on his chest. Even in her present prejudiced frame of mind, Cara had to admit that he was attractive. The hand he offered her was large and strong but well kept. She placed her own in it and found herself blushing when he held onto it. He smiled down at her, the blue eyes crinkling at the corners with a hint of challenge and as she caught the flash of white teeth a thought crossed her mind:

'He looks like a pirate!' 'How do you do, Mr O'Rourke. I see you've started without me,' she said pointedly.

The remark was completely lost on him. 'I've just taken some portrait shots of Janet,' he told her. 'I'll let you have a selection to choose from, don't worry. Now—what did you have in mind?'

Still annoyed, Cara opened her briefcase

8

and showed him her planned spread. He shook his head slowly, drawing his breath in through his teeth. 'I thought it was to be a feature on Janet's work—not her flat!' He looked at her. 'I mean—do you really think people are going to be interested in her kitchen?'

'Yes, I do,' Cara told him firmly, her cheeks reddening. 'Mine is a woman's magazine, don't forget. Our readers will be interested in Miss Lorimar's lifestyle as well as her work as a novelist.'

'Yes, but the *kitchen?*' He shook his head again. 'I thought today's woman liked to think of herself as liberated from things like that. I mean everyone knows what a kitchen looks like. I daresay a lot of your readers spend most of their lives in one. What they really want to see is her bedroom—her car—her collection of furs. The glamour of success.'

'I was planning to have those too!' Cara could feel her face going redder and redder as she stabbed a finger at the layout. How dare the man try to tell her her job? If Janet Lorimar hadn't been listening she would have told him to take a running jump at himself. As it was she satisfied her annoyance by saying: 'Look, I'll make a bargain with you, Mr O'Rourke. I won't try to teach you your job if you don't try to teach me mine!'

Janet Lorimar laughed. 'Good for you, my dear. And quite right too. Now, if you don't mind, I have a lunch date, so could we get on?'

By the time the session was through Cara felt like a limp rag. Nothing had turned out as she had planned it. O'Rourke overrode her every suggestion, determined to have everything his own way and with Janet Lorimar constantly looking at her watch the whole session was rushed. Cara had planned to have a picture of the novelist in the kitchen, wearing an apron, the theory being that the readers would identify with her. But O'Rourke insisted that the floating evening dress was more the expected image.

'Why not make your caption read: *"The Princess Of Passion Rustles Up A Love Potion?"*' he suggested wryly, watching Cara with folded arms.

'Thank you!' Cara shot him a venomous look. 'I think you can safely leave the captions with me!'

When they had finished Janet insisted on pouring them both a drink; then she went off to change for her lunch date. Cara sipped her gin and tonic gratefully, feeling she had deserved it. She watched O'Rourke putting away his equipment, her toe itching to aim a kick at the seat of his jeans as he bent over the case. As though he felt her eyes on him he turned and grinned.

'You know, you can never be too experienced to take good advice,' he told her patronisingly. 'I think you'll be pleased with my ideas. You know sometimes one can get too close to see things clearly. It takes an unjaundiced view to give you a fresh angle.'

Seething, Cara drained her glass and put it down smartly on the low table in front of her. 'I wasn't aware that my views were *jaundiced*! I take it you'll be willing to re-do any shots my editor doesn't like, by the way,' she said crisply. 'You see, she approved *my* layout. Yours might just conceivably not suit her, unjaundiced though it may be!' She raised an eyebrow at him. 'Incidentally, did you get in touch with Smithson and Browne's before you laid on this morning's session?'

He stared back at her blankly. 'Smithson and Browne's?'

Cara sighed. 'Miss Lorimar's publishers.'

He shook his head. 'I know who they are—but why should I contact them?'

'Because they insisted on being present at the interview,' she told him patiently.

He looked surprised. 'But this wasn't an interview, was it?' He straightened up. 'Well, that's that.' He looked at her. 'I suppose you're like all the rest—want to see the proofs yesterday!' He looked at his watch. 'I can get them round to your office later this afternoon—okay?' She nodded and he asked: 'Can I give you a lift anywhere?'

She was about to refuse until she noticed the time. At this rate she wouldn't get back to the office in time for her one o'clock lunch date with Anita. Although it went against the

11

grain to take anything from him she said reluctantly: 'Well—I—all right, thanks.'

'Great!' He snapped the case shut and thrust it into her hands. 'Might as well make yourself useful then. Carry this while I get the rest.'

Sitting beside him in the Bentley as it threaded its way through the busy lunchtime traffic Cara glanced at the powerful profile with its frame of chestnut hair. She caught herself wondering what he looked like under the beard. She had never trusted men with beards, or those who permanently hid behind dark glasses. They were a kind of disguise and, she considered, as such, suspect. He turned to glance at her.

'Anywhere special you'd like to eat?' he asked casually.

She looked at him blankly. How conceited could he get? Did he really expect her to have lunch with him—without even asking her properly? 'Sorry?' she said, feigning surprise.

'Lunch! Surely even features editors have to eat,' he said. 'Do you have a favourite place? If not, I think you'll like the one I have in mind . . .'

'Look, *I* think you take a damned sight too much for granted!' she told him indignantly. 'I happen to have a lunch date as it happens. That was the only reason I accepted your offer of a lift.' She glanced at her watch as they waited at a red light. 'I'm already late for it too.'

He glanced at her, the blue eyes glinting. 'In that case hold onto your seat!'

The ten minutes that followed were hair-raising as the Bentley swerved in and out of the heavy lunchtime traffic. Irate taxi drivers hooted and gestured rudely, indignant pedestrians shook their fists and leapt out of the way as O'Rourke launched the powerful green monster down side streets and round corners, before finally screeching to a halt outside the Imperial Magazines office block. Shaken, Cara got out onto the pavement to stand on jelly-like legs.

'Thanks for the lift. It was *quite* an experience!' she told him drily, determined not to let him see how terrified she had been.

He grinned. 'What's the point of having a car like this if you don't exploit its full potential?'

'Well, you get ten out of ten for doing *that*!' Cara told him.

He leaned across. 'Does your appreciation stretch to having dinner with me this evening?' he asked with the lift of an eyebrow.

She stared at him coldly. 'No way, O'Rourke! I've had enough of you for one day—you and your—your damned *pirate ship* here!' She kicked at one of the tyres, stubbing her toe painfully, then, turning, she walked into the building with as much dignity as she could manage, trying hard not to limp.

Upstairs in the office Jennifer Rogers, Anita's secretary, looked up from her desk.

'The chief's been looking for you,' she said. 'There was a phone call from Smithson and Browne's. They complained that you'd had a photographic session with Janet Lorimar without letting them know. They were pretty upset about it. Chief's gone to lunch. She told me to tell you she couldn't wait any longer.'

Cara groaned and looked at her watch. 'Oh no! That's all I need. I've had a hell of a morning. Has she gone to Mario's? Does she want me to join her there?'

Jennifer shook her head. 'No, her husband looked in so she went to lunch with him instead as you weren't back.'

Cara sank into a chair and kicked off her shoes. 'I just haven't the energy to go out for something to eat. I think I'll just sit here and expire peacefully.'

Jennifer laughed as she opened her desk drawer and took out a plastic box. Opening it she pushed it across the desk towards Cara. 'Here, share my sandwiches. I always make too many anyway.' She reached back into the drawer for a vacuum flask. 'There's plenty of coffee too. I loathe that dish water that comes out of the machine.' She unscrewed the top. 'Do you mind the flask top? I've only brought one cup.'

Cara accepted the drink and sandwich gratefully. As they munched, the other girl

14

looked at her. 'Well—what did you think of the notorious O'Rourke?'

Cara grimaced. 'Don't ask! The whole session was disaster from beginning to end. I knew there'd be trouble from Smithson and Browne's. And I've a feeling Anita isn't going to approve of the shots he took either.'

'But you had everything so carefully planned,' Jennifer said.

'Ah, but Mr O'Rourke knew better,' Cara told her bitterly. 'In his infinite wisdom he is convinced that our readers don't wish to see succesful women in the kitchen. They want to see them on pedestals—far above them— fantasy figures instead of someone they can identify with.'

Jennifer looked thoughtful. 'Maybe he has a point. After all, where's the joy in being successful if you still have to slave over a hot stove?' She laughed. 'Don't take it to heart so. There are only two kinds of woman in O'Rourke's book, anyway. Those he conquers with a look and those who take a little longer. And to him, both of them are the same in the end.'

Cara stopped in the act of biting a sandwich to stare at the other girl. 'You seem to know an awful lot about him.'

'I used to share a flat with a girl who was a model,' Jennifer explained. 'She worked with O'Rourke a lot—fell for him in a big way.'

'What happened?' Cara asked. She did her

15

best to sound casual but she found she was intrigued in spite of herself.

'She went the way of all the rest.' Jennifer shrugged. 'Tossed on the scrap-heap with all his old negatives.' She looked at Cara with interest. 'Did he make a pass at you?'

Cara snorted and stood up, brushing crumbs from her skirt. 'He seemed to take it for granted I'd have dinner with him. I soon put him right on that score! As for making a pass—I'd like to see him try!'

Jennifer laughed. 'Those sound suspiciously like famous last words.' She looked at Cara thoughtfully. 'Do you have a boyfriend, by the way? You never mention anyone. In fact you don't talk much about your private life at all.'

Cara laughed. 'Maybe that's because I don't really have one! At least not much of a one. I have to be the most boring person working for I.M.L. I used to share a flat with my mother, until she re-married and went to live in France. Now I live alone. I was educated at a girls' boarding school because my mother's career took up most of her time. That's about all there is. I love my job and I give most of my energy and attention to it.' She laughed at the other girl's expression. 'I told you I was boring—now you can see what I mean.'

'You still haven't answered the bit about boyfriends,' Jennifer reminded her.

Cara shrugged. 'You know how it is—the odd date here and there. Nothing serious. My

16

parents split up before I was born. It tends to give one a rather cynical view of marriage and the opposite sex.'

'You mean you don't really trust men?' Jennifer asked directly.

Cara grinned. 'You could say that.'

It was about halfway through the afternoon when she was summoned to Anita's office. The editor looked harassed.

'Where did you get to at lunch time?' As Cara opened her mouth to launch into an explanation she held up her hand. 'No—don't bother. It wouldn't have worked out anyhow. Look, it doesn't matter that you didn't let me know about your sudden change of plan, but I *do* wish you'd remembered to ring Smithson and Browne's. They were furious—seemed to think it was a put-up job. Apparently Janet tends to get a bit carried away once she starts talking. There have been one or two disastrous interviews in the past, of the kind they'd rather not repeat. That's why they put out the story about her being reclusive and also why they insist on being present at interviews.' Anita ran a hand through her short blonde hair. 'I had a hell of a job to persuade them not to cancel the whole thing.'

'I'm sorry. It didn't occur to me to ask O'Rourke if he'd contacted them until the session was over,' Cara told her. 'Even then I thought that as he's well in with them it'd be all right.'

Anita sighed wearily. 'You know the first rule in this business, Cara. Never take *anything* for granted. And don't rely on anyone except yourself—which brings me to this.' She pushed a large manilla envelope across the desk. 'They arrived about ten minutes ago and frankly I can't imagine what you were thinking about. These are more like pin-ups than shots of a novelist at work. I'm afraid they'll all have to be done again.'

Cara slumped dejectedly. 'I was afraid you'd say that.'

Anita removed her glasses to look earnestly at her features editor. 'Are you feeling all right, Cara? You're looking rather tired.'

'I'm fine—really. It's just—well, O'Rourke lived up to the stories about him. He *is* difficult to work with. He simply took over—tossed all my ideas out of the window and insisted on doing it all from his own angle.'

Anita stared at her. 'But you shouldn't have *let* him! Look, this work will all have to be done again and the budget won't stretch to two sessions, not at O'Rourke's prices. I'm afraid you're going to have to ring him and tell him so, Cara. And the sooner the better.'

Cara froze inwardly. To have to ring the man—and plead with him over something that was his fault in the first place ... 'Yes—of course,' she said, swallowing hard. 'I'll do it right away.' She got up and walked towards the door but as she began to open it Anita spoke again:

'And Cara . . .'

'Yes?'

'Don't be so abrasive. Try being nice to him. Butter him up a little. After all, he *is* a man.' She smiled. 'You might be very surprised at the results.'

Cara closed the door and pulled a face at it. Of all the humiliations! It was bad enough to have to ask him to do the session again, but to have to *be nice* to him after the trouble he had caused her. Oh well . . . She squared her shoulders. Better get it over with as soon as possible, she supposed. On her way through she asked Jennifer to get him on the line for her. She had been at her desk a few moments when the telephone rang. Jennifer's voice said:

'Mr O'Rourke on the line for you, Cara.'

She cleared her throat and spoke: 'Good afternoon—Mr O'Rourke.'

'Cara—what can I do for you? Did the proofs arrive safely?'

She took a deep breath to try to steady her quickened heartbeat. Really, it was ridiculous. The man deserved everything she was going to say. He could hardly refuse to take the shots again—could he? 'They did. That's what I'm calling you about. I'm afraid my editor isn't pleased with them. I did try to tell you, Mr O'Rourke. I . . .'

'Corin,' he interrupted.

She frowned into the receiver. 'What?'

'Please—call me Corin,' he repeated 'Or just plain O'Rourke if you like. When you say "Mr" I keep thinking you're talking to someone respectable! Now—the proofs—what's the problem?'

'I'm sorry, they're not what we wanted.'

'Then why didn't you say so?' he asked innocently.

Oh! He *must* know how annoying he was being! 'I did!' Cara's voice rose shrilly and she bit off the sentence abruptly, biting her lip as she remembered Anita's advice. 'I did try to make my ideas clear to you, Mr—er, Corin,' she said with studied calm. 'You see, it's the policy of this magazine to boost the confidence of the woman at home. To make her feel that anything is possible and that all women, from the M.P. and the famous film star down to the housewife and mum have basically the same potential.'

The laughter that crackled the line made her wince and hold the receiver away from her ear. She waited a moment, determined not to be rattled by what she saw as an attempt to goad her. 'So will you do the shots again—please?' she said with cool determination.

'Well—since you ask so prettily—yes, on one condition.'

She groaned inwardly, guessing what was coming. 'And what would that be?'

'That you have dinner with me tonight.'

Cara stared helplessly into the receiver.

20

So—he had won after all. For one fleeting moment she was tempted to see what would happen if she refused, then she decided that she didn't have the nerve. 'Well—all right,' she said slowly.

'Good.' The triumph was plain to hear in his voice. 'I'll pick you up at about half-past eight. 'Bye, Cara.'

'Wait! I haven't told you where I live . . .' she began. But she was speaking to an empty line. He had already rung off.

CHAPTER TWO

As Cara came out of the office the sun was shining for the first time that day. She decided to take a leisurely walk down The Strand and look at the river before catching the train. Passing the Duke's Theatre she glanced at the photographs displayed outside and read the notices: *Clive Redway in 'Goodnight, Miss Jones.' Smash hit goes into second year! Redway is ripping in this twenties revival!*

On a sudden impulse Cara slipped round to the stage door and went in. The stage door keeper grinned at her from his cubbyhole.

'Evening, Miss Dean.'

'Hello, Bert. Is Mr Redway in?'

'Yes, Miss. Curtain came down about twenty minutes ago.'

Cara walked down the corridor and tapped on the door of dressing-room number one. A deep, resonant voice bade her enter. Clive Redway was sitting at the dressing table, busily removing his make-up. He wore a blue silk dressing gown that was the exact colour of his eyes and his fair, wavy hair was ruffled, giving him the vulnerable, boyish look he was famous for. When he looked up and saw Cara through the mirror his handsome face broke immediately into a broad smile.

'Darling, how lovely! To what do I owe this unexpected pleasure?'

Cara closed the door and went across the room to drop a kiss on his forehead. 'I was passing the theatre and I had a sudden desire to see my favourite actor.'

'I'm so glad you did, darling. You're looking marvellous. Look, wait till I've washed and changed and I'll take you out to a meal before the evening show—unless of course you've got to rush off.'

Cara shook her head. 'I'm sorry, Clive, I have as a matter of fact. I have a dinner date. This big-headed photographer messed up my whole day's work and I have orders to plead with him to do the session again.' She ruffled his hair. 'You know I'd far rather have dinner with you.'

Clive sighed and hurriedly removed the rest of his make-up. 'What a bore for you. Never mind. We'll have an early drink. Or if you like

Briggs will pop out for some of those ruinous cream cakes you adore and make us some tea. Then we can have it here, just the two of us, all nice and cosy. What do you say?'

Cara smiled, pretending not to notice how relieved he was that she hadn't taken up his invitation to go out to dinner with him. It was a kind of game they played. He regularly asked her and she regularly made an excuse. Secretly, each knew they could rely on the other to play their part, though Cara often wished he would come right out in the open and tell her he didn't want to be seen in public with her.

At Clive's shout, Briggs put his head round the door. He was a small, wiry man with a sad-comic face and a broad cockney accent. He grinned when he saw Cara, his kind brown eyes lighting up.

'Miss Dean. Smashing! I'm glad you popped in. We've been feeling a bit grouchy today!' He nodded pointedly at the back of Clive's head. 'Got out of the wrong side of someone's bed, I shouldn't wonder.'

Clive shook his head impatiently. 'Oh, belt up, you old fool! Cara doesn't want to hear your homespun platitudes. Look, slip out and get us some of those cream cakes from the Green Dragon, then make us some tea. China, mind!' he called to Briggs' retreating back. 'None of your nasty Indian stand-the-spoon-up-in-the-cup rubbish!'

23

Cara laughed. 'You're so *rude* to each other. Anyone who didn't know you both would wonder why he stayed.'

'Huh! Knows which side his bread's buttered,' Clive said.

'And that goes for you too. You'd be lost without Briggs and you know it,' Cara told him.

Clive went across to the wash-basin and rinsed away the last traces of make-up, turning to her with a smile. 'You know me pretty well, don't you?' He sighed as he threw down the towel and sat down again, crossing one leg over the other and lighting a cigarette. He looked at her appreciatively. 'When I think of the time I wasted. All those years when I didn't even know you existed!'

Cara looked at him ruefully. She would never quite get used to the change in his appearance after the removal of his stage make-up. It was a metamorphosis—from heart-throb to man-in-the-street in thirty seconds flat. She much preferred the man-in-the-street.

'That goes for me too. Was Briggs right about you being grouchy?'

He pulled a face. 'Isn't he always, damn him?' He flicked ash from his cigarette. 'It's this bloody play. It's been running too long. I always get restless during a long run.' He blew out a cloud of smoke and gave her a slightly desperate, over-bright smile through it. 'Still—

24

mustn't grumble, must I? At least I'm working at the moment. One of these days I'll be lucky to get a part at all.' The smile slipped. 'There are days when I feel that time isn't too far distant and this is one of them.'

'Oh dear—you *are* depressed. You must have been sending out a telepathic S.O.S. to me as I passed the theatre,' Cara said. 'Never mind—cream cakes and China tea will cheer you up.'

'I doubt it. To tell you the truth my agent hasn't had an enquiry for me for months. This play will run for another six weeks at the most by the look of the advance bookings. After that . . .' He stubbed out his cigarette forcibly. 'Yours truly Clive Redway could find himself in for a long period of *resting.*'

'Oh dear. You usually have something lined up, don't you?' Cara said, feeling helpless. 'I wish there was something I could do.'

Suddenly he reached out to take both of her hands. 'Bless you, darling. You really mean that, don't you? Listen, Cara, I know neither of us has ever actually mentioned it—not in so many words, but you do understand why I haven't wanted to make the relationship between us public, don't you? I know you deserve better.' He squeezed her hands tightly. 'But quite soon now I'm going to do something about that—make it all up to you.'

Cara smiled understandingly. 'There's no need for you to feel like that. It doesn't matter a bit, people not knowing. Just as long as I can see you occasionally.'

He looked at her earnestly. 'But I mean it. I've made up my mind. You and I are going to be seen about together and to hell with the wretched news-hounds!' He shot her a rueful, apologetic smile. 'Oh—sorry love. That was tactless.'

She laughed. 'I'm not a news-hound, silly!'

He looked at her. 'You do know I love you, don't you, darling?'

'Of course—and I love you too. I always will, so don't worry.'

He gave her the famous smile. 'Anyway, enough about me. What about you? Are you happy? I mean—you always seem to work too hard. You ought to get out more—enjoy yourself . . .'

She disengaged her hands. 'Clive. If you're going to worry about me like this I shall have to stop seeing you,' she told him firmly. 'I'm perfectly all right. I love my job and I have my own life, so let's not talk about it any more.'

An hour later Cara was on her way home, leaving Clive to prepare for the evening performance. When it was time for her to leave Briggs had walked to the stage door with her. In the narrow little side street the air was mellow, made heavy with the nostalgic scent of wallflowers that someone had thoughtfully planted in a tub near the door. They drowned the faint odour of drains stirred up by the

26

earlier rain. Spring had even managed to penetrate this dark little alleyway and Cara sniffed appreciatively, thinking longingly of the country and Clive's cottage in the Cotswolds where she had spent the odd idyllic weekend with him.

'Thanks for looking in,' Briggs said, his wrinkled little face anxious. 'He was having one of his bad days. He always get depressed when the offers don't flood in. His agent's been negotiating for a part in a film for him. Quite thought it was in the bag, but it fell through. He heard this morning. Then there's the image. Keeping up the reputation of being a "hell raiser" gets harder as the years go by, I reckon.' He grinned at her. 'Still, the sight of you always does him a power of good.'

'I wish I could do more,' Cara told him wistfully. 'It makes me so sad, not being able to tell people that he's my father.'

*   *   *

As she rattled homewards on the underground she closed her eyes, letting her mind go back to that day when she was seventeen—the day she began her course in journalism—the day that her mother had told her for the first time that the father she had believed dead all these years was, in fact, not only alive but well-known to thousands of people.

Clive Redway, the actor, was as famous for

his appearances in the gossip columns as in the theatre. There was always a different girl on his arm, most of them as well-known as himself. They ranged from beauty-queens and actresses to ladies from the minor aristocracy. Age seemed no barrier either. He had been known to escort women from seventeen to fifty. From the accounts of the wild parties he gave and attended it seemed that Clive had no intention of relinquishing his unofficial title of hell-raiser extraordinaire even though he was well into his middle years.

Cara had never doubted the story her mother had fabricated for her—that her father had left before she was born and had later been killed in an accident, so the revelation that she was the product of a hasty and disastrous marriage when Clive and her mother had been in provincial rep. together had come as a shock. Finding herself about to marry again after so many years, Sarah Dean had at last faced the fact that she owed her daughter the truth.

'It's up to you what you do about it,' she had said after her shattering confession. 'If you take my advice you'll stay away from him. He's never meant anything but trouble for the women in his life and I doubt very much if you'd be any exception. You'll probably only be an embarrassment to him, anyway.'

But Cara couldn't rest until she had at least made the acquaintance of the man to whom

28

she owed her existence. As a child she had made up her own private fantasies about her shadowy father, a mythical character made romantic by the mystery that surrounded him and she couldn't resist finding out just how close to the truth her fantasies had been.

She had expected someone entirely different from the man she now knew. Once he had got to know her, Clive had dropped his guard. The glossy outward shell he allowed the world to see crumbled to reveal the real man inside, vulnerable and childishly naive at times; secretly afraid of approaching age and hanging on desperately to the last vestiges of youth. Although she could see that everything her mother had told her about him was true, she found him magnetic and appealing, maddening and lovable, all at the same time and they had been firm if secret friends ever since.

Cara's existence had come as no less of a shock to Clive. He had left Sarah before she had had time to tell him she was pregnant. But after he had recovered from the initial blow he had been touchingly delighted to find that he had a daughter and anxious for them to remain in touch. Without a word ever being spoken on the subject, Cara had sensed quite quickly that a daughter might well be an embarrassment as her mother had predicted. She had known instinctively that he was reluctant for their relationship to be made public. Until this evening he had never actually said it in so many words. It had remained an unspoken rule that neither of them would break. Cara wondered what had prompted him to come out into the open with it at last, and what he had meant when he had spoken of their being seen together and about 'making it all up to her.'

*   *   *

As she let herself into the flat she looked at her watch and saw with a shock that it was a quarter to eight. She would have to hurry if she was to be ready when O'Rourke called for her. She quickly undressed and showered, pulling on a dressing gown and opening the wardrobe to survey her clothes. She had no idea where O'Rourke would take her. Looking at him this morning it was impossible to evaluate his tastes in anything, let alone eating places. It might be anything from the Savoy to an East End fish and chip shop.

After some thought she finally chose a plain black velvet skirt and white silk shirt, adding a pair of jade earrings as an afterthought just in case.

He arrived on time, which surprised her, and she was further surprised to see that he was dressed quite formally. The jeans and leather jacket of this morning having given way to a well-cut grey suit, complete with neat tie and waistcoat. But even with his hair and beard well brushed he still had the look of a buccaneer to Cara. She gave him a drink and asked him to wait in her small sitting room while she finished getting ready. Peering at him through the half-open door she thought he looked slightly menacing—filling her small living room with his bulk. He looked like a large well-fed tiger, waiting to pounce on its unsuspecting prey. She made up her mind there and then that the prey would not be called Cara Dean!

He took her to a trendy restaurant that had once been a potato warehouse in a partly redeveloped area south of the river. It had scrubbed tables and cane chairs and the stairs to the first floor were barely more than a ladder. But the food and wine were excellent and by the look of the clientèle it was obviously a fashionable place. On their way to their table O'Rourke was stopped several times to be greeted warmly and affectionately by glamorous women who, he explained lightly to her as they settled themselves at the table, were 'colleagues' with whom he often worked.

During the first course O'Rourke tried to find out more about her and failed. All she was prepared to talk about was her job; after all, that was all that concerned him. She was just about to tell him so when he switched the subject abruptly to the morning's photographic session with Janet Lorimar.

'You know, you really should have put your foot down with a firm hand this morning,' he told her, flashing the disarming smile. 'I tend to get carried away when I photograph beautiful women and Janet is rather gorgeous, even if she is pushing forty.' He cocked an expressive eyebrow at her. 'Don't you agree?'

Cara stared at him, wondering what would actually have happened if she had put her foot down, as he put it. She felt certain that he would have taken no notice. After all, she *had* tried to tell him she knew what she wanted. 'Certainly,' she said in answer to his question about Janet's looks. 'She's very attractive.'

'Of course, she's a complete eccentric,' O'Rourke went on. 'Totally wrapped up in her writing. Anyone who didn't know her would think she was bananas. One or two of the hacks who have interviewed her have made her sound distinctly wacky, poor love.' He looked at her with narrowed eyes. 'I hope you won't do that.'

'Naturally not.' Cara looked at the strong face, trying to read its defensive expression. Was he in love with Janet Lorimar, she wondered? Was he setting himself up as her minder? 'And just for the record, I'm *not* a hack,' she told him. 'Now—when can you do those re-takes for me?'

He studied her face for a moment, a smile twitching the corners of his mouth, then he took out a diary and consulted it for a moment, stroking his beard thoughtfully. 'Well—I might be able to squeeze it in a week next Friday.'

'*A week on Friday?* But that's ten days from now!' Cara exploded. 'I can't wait till then. I have a deadline to meet. The feature has to coincide with the launching of Janet's new book, don't forget.'

Totally unmoved by her display of outraged impatience he put away the diary and cast an eye over the sweet-trolley which the waiter had just wheeled up. 'Well now, will you just look at this tempting array! What will you have? The crème caramel looks good.' He cast a speculative eye over what he could see of her figure. 'Or are you counting calories?'

'Nothing more for me, thank you,' Cara said, tight-lipped as she tapped her foot impatiently under the table. Irritation mounted inside her as he took his time choosing a sweet from the selection on the trolley. He seemed to be deliberately ignoring her obvious concern over her deadline. When at last the waiter had moved on to the next table she hissed at him:

'Did you hear what I said? Surely you can manage an hour before a week on Friday?'

O'Rourke glanced up at her from under the thick eyebrows as he tucked into his strawberry Pavlova with obvious relish. 'Let me give you a valuable tip, Cara,' he said calmly. 'Talking business over food is the worst thing one can do for the digestion.' He shook his head at her. 'Gives you an ulcer quicker than anything.'

'That's why I'm not eating!' she told him caustically.

'Ah, but *I* am.' He smiled calmly. 'And this is as light as thistledown—much too good to spoil by fretting about deadlines. Now, suppose we discuss the whole thing over coffee—at my place?'

'Can't we just have coffee and talk about it here?' Cara's patience was almost at snapping point but she bit back the sharp, sarcastic comments that chased each other round her fuming mind, longing to be voiced. After all, she was relying on this man and she daren't allow herself the luxury of forgetting it.

He pushed away his clean plate, dabbing at his lips with his napkin and waving to another dazzling beauty who had just come in. 'It's getting much too crowded to talk properly here,' he told her. 'Besides, I have a more detailed diary at my studio.'

She regarded the handsome face, trying to gauge whether he was just stringing her along. Looking at her watch she said:

'I can give you till ten-thirty, no longer. I have some work waiting for me at home.'

He caught the eye of the waiter and beckoned him over, a look of amusement lifting the corners of his mouth as he turned his attention back to her. 'Really? Till ten-thirty, eh? Well, if I work fast I think we should be able to make it in that time.' His eyes were openly challenging as he looked steadily at her across the table.

As the audacious blue eyes met hers she felt hot colour rise in her cheeks. Really! He needn't be quite so obvious! Annoyed with herself for being dumbfounded by such an unsubtle approach, she gathered up her bag and muttered an excuse, leaving him to pay the bill while she escaped to the cloakroom.

O'Rourke's studio was in a quiet Chelsea mews and, as Cara had guessed, it was also his home. Leaving the car in the little cobbled alley he unlocked the white-painted front door for her, holding it so that she could enter ahead of him. A flight of stairs led to a large, untidy room that seemed to serve as a living room. Two steps led to a large, airy studio with an enormous south-facing window. It was littered with photographic equipment. Tidiness quite clearly wasn't O'Rourke's forte.

He looked at her, rubbing his hands. 'Right—first things first. Coffee. Black or white? Or perhaps you'd rather have a drink?' He took off his jacket and threw it over the back of a chair.

She shrugged, standing squarely in the centre of the large room. Might as well let him know she was here for one thing and one thing only. 'You don't have to make coffee for me,' she told him firmly. 'All I'm really concerned about is the date for this session with Janet.'

He had walked across to the doorway, but now he turned, leaning against the jamb to look at her speculatively, arms folded. 'You said you could give me until ten-thirty,' he reminded her, one eyebrow raised lazily. 'That gives us almost an hour. How did you intend us to fill the rest of the time, I wonder?'

He was laughing at her. Making her feel like a gauche teenager and she resented it. It was his fault that this morning's session had been spoilt. He had no right to play silly games—amuse himself with her in this infantile way. He must have seen that she was angry because he suddenly became serious, straightening up and moving across the room towards her.

'I'm sorry, Cara,' he said. 'I'm only teasing, you know. I can't resist it. You bring out the devil in me with that fiercely determined look of yours.' He stood before her, looking down into her eyes. Cupping her chin with one large hand, he studied her face. 'Why do you take yourself so seriously?' he asked her. 'For heaven's sake relax. Life's a ball if you'll only let it be.'

As the deep blue eyes looked into hers something odd happened. Her confidence suddenly left her and just for a moment she felt as though she could neither move nor speak. Her heart began to beat unevenly and she found she was short of breath as she stammered:

'I—I really should go. Can—can we just

36

look at your diary and fix a date—please?'

'Of course we will—in a minute.' His voice was soothing and the hand that cupped her chin moved down her neck and slipped inside the neck of her shirt, the fingers caressing her collarbone. 'You're so tense. I can feel every muscle,' he observed. 'What's the matter, Cara? You're not afraid of me, are you?'

She swallowed hard and gave a dry, forced little laugh. 'Afraid of *you*! Certainly not! Look—I came here with you to try to fix a date for that session. Not to talk about my alleged aversions and the state of my muscles!' She was aware that she was trembling and silently cursed herself for her lack of control. She was acutely and disturbingly aware of the warmth of his hand on her neck and the little pulse that fluttered at the base of her throat under his stroking thumb. But his shrewd, frankly disbelieving eyes held hers almost hypnotically and there wasn't a thing she could do about it. Suddenly his hand slipped round to the back of her neck, the fingers twining into her hair. As he pulled her towards him his other arm slid round her waist and his mouth swiftly covered hers, holding her head in a vice-like grip so that she couldn't escape. She resisted with a sudden blaze of anger at the way it was done—almost a violation! She even lifted one foot to kick his shin, then as his lips moved against hers she found herself capitulating helplessly. Afterwards she found it impossible

37

to analyse just what had happened. His beard brushed roughly against her face, yet his mouth was smooth and warm, tender and searching, his lips gently coaxing hers apart, caressing and exploring until she relaxed weakly against him and gave herself up to the engulfing sensuality of his kiss.

At last he released her, framing her face with his hands to smile down at her with darkened eyes that gleamed with a hint of triumph.

'There—that's better. Now—about that session.' He left her standing there, walking away into the studio to rummage in a drawer while she stood, swaying slightly, suddenly bereft of his support, trying desperately to bring her wildly stirred emotions under some kind of control again.

He returned with a large desk diary and sat down to open it. She stared at him. It was almost as though the kiss had never happened. He certainly seemed unmoved by it as he ran a finger down the dates in the diary. 'Mmm— you're doing the interview tomorrow. If everything goes according to schedule I could come round and re-do the shots at about five o'clock. It'll be a mad rush of course—but for you . . .' He looked up at her and his eyebrows rose. 'What is it? Are you all right?'

She pulled herself together with an effort. 'Yes—of course. I—er—thank you.' *Damn him!* She wouldn't let him see that the kiss had thrown her. Obviously he was used to kissing any female who happened to take his fancy—*and* to having his kiss returned and accepted for what it was, a casual gesture at the end of a pleasant evening. He thought nothing of it—and neither should she. It was too absurd to react like this! She took a deep breath and forced herself to smile, hoping she looked calmer than she felt.

'That would suit me very well.' She looked at her watch. 'I'll see you at Janet Lorimar's tomorrow afternoon, then. I really should go now. I told you, I do still have some work to do for tomorrow.'

He stood up, tossing the diary aside and picking up his jacket. 'Okay. I'll take you.'

She spun round, a feeling of panic making her heart race. 'No! I—I'll be all right. I can easily get the Tube.'

For a second he stared at her, his eyes widening at the shrill note in her voice. Then he smiled. 'Nonsense! I wouldn't dream of letting you go home alone.' He pulled on the jacket and took her arm, propelling her firmly out through the door. 'Never let it be said that O'Rourke lets his ladies go home alone! I have a reputation to keep up, remember?'

She was silent as they drove across London and when he drew the Bentley to a halt outside her flat and she made to open the door he put out a hand to stop her, looking at her with puzzled eyes.

'Cara—what did I do?'

'Sorry?' Her hand trembled as she clutched at the door handle. She didn't trust herself to look at him.

'There's something wrong. Come on, what is it? Did I say something?'

She carefully detached his hand from her arm. 'Of course you didn't. Look, I have to go, O'Rourke. I told you—I have work to do. I'll see you tomorrow.' She turned, half out of the car. 'Oh—er—thank you for the dinner.'

He shrugged, an amused smile on his face. 'Don't mention it!'

She watched from the shadow of the doorway as the car's red rear lights disappeared, then drew a long breath. Thank goodness for that! Tomorrow she would time her interview so that she was clear of Janet Lorimar's flat before he arrived. She would leave a detailed list of the pictures she wanted and see that Janet was wearing the right clothes before she left. She was forced to admit that she found O'Rourke's presence far too disturbing to make any further meetings with him advisable. She could do without that kind of complication in her life!

CHAPTER THREE

From the moment Cara began to interview Janet Lorimar she could see how an unscrupulous reporter could have a field day, especially the kind who despised popular fiction and women writers in particular. The novelist tended to get lost in a fantasy world peopled with the characters from her books so that it was difficult for the listener to separate fact from fiction. When she announced that it was her housekeeper's day off and went to organise tea Dorcas Fairfield, Janet's editor from Smithson and Browne's, glanced at Cara and drew a sigh.

'Thank God you're the sensible type,' she said. 'You should have read the last interview. It was in one of the more garish popular dailies and it made her sound like a raving loony—as for T.V. chat shows—the very thought makes my blood run cold!' She rolled her eyes ceilingwards, leaving the rest to Cara's imagination.

'I can see that quoting her out of context might make for interesting reading to say the least,' Cara said guardedly. 'She's so absorbed with her characters you feel she thinks of them as totally real, almost as though they were members of her own family. By the way, I'm sorry about yesterday. As it happens O'Rourke is going to do the photographs again. I'm afraid I let him have his head and my editor wasn't best pleased with the results.'

Dorcas brushed aside the apology. 'Poor you! Of course it wouldn't have happened if I'd been here,' she said. 'I'm used to working with him and I know how to curb his enthusiasm.'

Taking a look at the business-like, horn-rimmed spectacles, tailored suit and sensible shoes, Cara could well believe it. She was obviously a very single-minded lady who knew just what she wanted and how to get it.

'When is he coming?' Dorcas went on. 'I'll make a point of being here next time to see that you don't have any more trouble.'

'This afternoon at about five,' Cara told her. 'I wasn't planning to be here. I thought I'd leave a list of what I wanted. So if you're going to be here . . .'

'Damn! I can't!' Dorcas snapped her fingers. 'Got a train to catch at four. Our latest thriller writer lives in Cumbria and he hates coming south, so I've got to go up there to discuss the storyline for his next book.' Dorcas gave a warning shake of her head. 'I wouldn't give Corin a free hand again if I were you. He picks up atmosphere, you see, like the true artist he is. He can't help himself. It's that ethereal look of Janet's. Before you know where you are he'll be posing her draped over a *chaise-longue* swathed in pink tulle with a rose in her teeth! And all your plans for portraying her as a hardworking career woman will have gone up in a cloud of Chanel Number 5!'

Cara couldn't help laughing at Dorcas's turn of phrase. 'Maybe you're right. I'd better make a point of being here after all, I suppose.' But even as she said the words her heart gave an involuntary lurch.

Dorcas disposed of the tea Janet poured her in double quick time, then briskly gathered up her handbag and briefcase.

'Well, have to love you and leave you, I'm afraid,' she announced. 'Got to go home and pack a few things. I expect to be away for at least two days.' She looked at Cara. 'I'm sure I can leave you to do the rest. I've warned you about being firm with Corin and I think you've got all you want for the interview, haven't you?'

Cara nodded. 'All I need now are the details of the rooms we want to show—Janet's study and so on. Colour schemes.' She looked at the author. 'Miss Lorimar has kindly agreed to my taking notes on those before I leave.'

When Dorcas had gone Janet came back into the room and sank onto the settee wearily.

'Oh dear. Dorcas is a dear but rather overwhelming, don't you find?' She smiled at Cara. 'You're a much more restful person.' She leaned forward, one hand on the teapot. 'Shall

43

we have another cup before we start again?'

'Thank you.' Cara accepted the tea Janet handed her. 'I'm sorry the photographs all have to be done again. I'm afraid it was all my fault really.' A glimmer of hope began to rear its head. 'Look, if you're too tired I could always arrange to postpone . . .'

Janet stopped her with a wave of her hand. 'Not at all, my dear. Might as well get it all over with in one go. I'm only sorry you have to work late.' She held up her cup. 'This will do wonders for me. It always does.'

As they toured the flat Cara took careful notes, paying special attention to the study. It was a delight with its book-lined walls and antique desk. Soft green velvet curtains hung at the windows, which faced the park.

'Isn't it beautiful?' Janet said, looking out. 'Everything bursting into bloom. Who could help waxing lyrical?'

But Cara was more interested in something she had seen lying on the desk. It was a manuscript, this time not a romantic novel but a T.V. play. She was just wondering whether to draw attention to it when Janet turned and saw her looking at it.

'Ah, you've seen my new baby! I meant to put that away.'

Cara had stolen a look at the first page, fascinated to see that it was a complete departure for the woman thousands knew as the 'Princess of Passion.' She looked up.

44

'I love the title—*Buds In Winter*. Will it be screened soon?'

Janet Lorimar lifted her shoulders. 'So far, apart from my agent only one other person knows about it. I haven't even told Dorcas. As you know, my ex-husband is a T.V. director. We're still very good friends. He's extremely interested in it, but up to now that's as far as it's gone.' She took the manuscript from Cara. 'It could be a little difficult to cast. You see the main character is an ageing actor trying to come to terms with the fact that he's past his best.' She smiled wryly. 'Actors being the vain creatures they are, that could pose a problem.'

Cara's heart suddenly quickened but she tried to sound casual as she said: 'I can think of one actor who'd play the part perfectly.'

'Oh, and who is that?'

'Clive Redway.'

Janet laughed. 'Ah, well, now you're talking! I agree absolutely, but he's quite a notorious playboy and with a reputation like his I'm afraid he might consider it damaging to his image! He . . .' A sudden shrilling of the front door bell made her stop what she was about to say. 'Ah—that will be Corin. I'll go and let him in.' She paused in the doorway to look back at Cara over her shoulder. 'Oh—by the way, I hope I can rely on you not to print anything in your magazine about that.' She nodded towards the manuscript on the desk.

Cara met her eyes gravely. 'Naturally. You

have my word on it.'

Today O'Rourke was cooperative. He worked briskly and efficiently, with the quiet precision of the true professional, taking the photographs exactly as Cara stipulated without passing any more of his own opinions. The session was soon over and as he packed away his equipment he glanced at her.

'Are you all right?'

Her heart lurched. 'Of course. Why do you ask?' she asked defensively.

He held up his hands. 'No reason—except that when I left you last night you seemed . . .' He paused, choosing his words carefully. 'Preoccupied, shall we say?'

She did her best to sound cool. 'I—I had a lot on my mind.'

'Anything to do with me? I mean, was it something I did?'

'You've already asked me that. I can't think of anything you've done that would cause me to be preoccupied,' she told him caustically. 'Unless you count yesterday's abortive session here.'

'Well, I think you'll agree that I've made up for that now.' He snapped his case shut and looked at her as he pulled on his black leather jacket. 'Doing anything special?'

'When?'

'Right now. I have to do a set of fashion shots in Kensington Gardens. They're to be taken at dusk. It's a feature for "Fashion

46

2,000." And it's to be titled Midsummer-Night's Dream. I just thought it might interest you, that's all.'

She searched her mind for an excuse that didn't sound feeble. 'But—it won't be dusk for another couple of hours.'

He grinned at her. 'I know. But we could fill the time in eating—or something.'

Cara hesitated, trying hard to conquer the panic that quickened her heartbeat. Then inspiration struck. 'I'd rather you used the time developing those new shots so that I could take the proofs in to the office with me in the morning,' she said.

His eyebrows shot up. 'You don't ask much, do you?'

'I'm not my editor's favourite person at the moment,' she told him. 'If I could show up complete with the new set of proofs tomorrow morning I might get back into her good books again. I—think you owe me that.'

He grinned, looking more piratical than ever. 'I see. Okay, so what's it worth?'

She stared at him. 'Worth?'

'Come now, you don't expect me to work overtime and go without my dinner for nothing, do you?'

'I—could see if I could wangle another fee for you,' she said, deliberately misunderstanding. 'But I don't hold out much hope. You see . . .'

He chuckled disarmingly and Janet coming

47

back into the room after changing, wanted to know what the joke was.

'This lady has the cheek to expect me to go without my dinner to produce proofs for her, just so that she can impress her editor!' he supplied, making Cara's colour rise. '*Me*—the great O'Rourke!' There was a hint of granite in the blue eyes as he added: 'I didn't get where I am today by doing *favours* for people, sweetheart! And I don't allow people to use me—however attractive they might be.'

Chastened, she stood silently beside him in the lift on the way down. O'Rourke whistled casually, but his anger filled the small space, crackling the air like electricity. As the lift hummed to a halt he stopped whistling abruptly and shot her a look.

'Right—I'll make a bargain with you. You get the take-away while I set to work.'

'Oh no, it's all right.' She made to step out of the lift as the doors opened, but he grabbed her arm, holding her against the side of the lift in an iron grip. 'You do the washing-up too, mind? *And* make the coffee afterwards. Then—if you're good—I'll let you help me with the Midsummer-Night's Dream session. Do we have a deal?'

She looked up into the glittering eyes. She never could tell when he was laughing at her and when he was serious. Every instinct she had urged her to tell him to go to hell, but she *did* want those proofs for the morning. The tip

48

of her tongue came out to moisten lips that felt suddenly dry. 'Okay,' she said. 'You're on. I'll call the office and let them know I won't be back.'

At the studio he went straight into his dark room whilst Cara went in search of somewhere to buy fast food. She found an Indian restaurant about a hundred yards down the street and ordered chicken Tandoori for two, hoping it would be to O'Rourke's liking. On her way she had spotted a delicatessen and off-licence and on the way back she bought cheese and biscuits and a bottle of wine to complete the meal.

Back at the studio she searched for cutlery and a table cloth and laid the table in the window that looked out over the cobbled alley with its blossoming window boxes and trees in tubs, then she plugged in the coffee filter in O'Rourke's small littered kitchen, putting away various packets and utensils as she did so.

'My God! I thought for a moment I'd strayed into the wrong flat!' O'Rourke had wandered in quietly and stood behind her, looking around him. 'I'll never be able to find a thing now! Why is it that women can never resist organising things?'

'I don't know how anyone can work in this muddle,' she complained. 'It's supposed to be a reflection of a person's character, you know. I'd be careful who I allowed to see it if I were

49

you. If an analyst were to see this place I don't know what he'd make of you!'

'And what makes you so sure that the muddle is mine?' he asked teasingly.

She turned to look at him as he leant against the worktop, arms folded, head on one side. It was impossible to read his expression from those enigmatic eyes. Damn that beard! She felt the warm colour slowly rise up her neck to flush her cheeks. It had never occurred to her that he might not live alone.

'Oh!—I assumed . . .'

'Now *that's* a character flaw in you,' he told her, pointing an accusing finger. 'You *assume* too much. For all you know I might have a live-in girlfriend—even a wife!'

She swallowed. 'And have you?'

The expressive eyebrows rose a fraction. 'You're the character expert. You tell me.'

She took a deep breath, determined not to be thrown. 'If you have, I'd say she hasn't been around for some time. I can't believe that any woman would let a beautiful flat like this get into such a mess.'

'Well, I'm glad you approve of the flat at least!' He turned and began to take the foil cartons out of their carrier bag, lifting a corner of one lid to sniff at the contents. 'Now, what have we here? Aaah—chicken Tandoori. So you're a mind reader too?'

'I got some wine to go with it; dry, white. And cheese to follow,' she told him, wondering

50

why he had changed the subject so abruptly.

He glanced up. 'A nice ripe Stilton, I hope?'

She shook her head. 'Brie. I thought a mildish one after the Tandoori.'

He shrugged and began to spoon the food onto plates. 'Ah well—fair enough. I can't expect perfection every time, can I?'

He ate his food quickly but with relish, then took his coffee back into the darkroom with him, announcing that they would have to leave for Kensington Gardens in twenty minutes. Cara washed up, then, to fill the time, did a little more tidying, in the living room this time, looking at the contents of his bookcase as she went. She was surprised at what she found. Annotated copies of Shakespeare plays sat side by side with paperback thrillers; on the shelf below, anthologies of twentieth century poets. Wilfred Owen, Rupert Brooke and Siegfried Sassoon. Not at all what she had expected. She picked up a handful of cassettes that lay on the shelf above the stereo and glanced at the titles. Two were of heavy rock groups—the third, a collection of the music of Delius. Clearly, O'Rourke was a man of varied tastes. She wondered if that went for his taste in women too! At least O'Rourke had made no attempt to make a pass at her this evening.

Finding the bathroom she repaired her make-up and ran a comb through her long dark hair. Standing close to the mirror she scrutinised her face. The wide-set brown eyes looked back critically. She had good bone structure, she supposed, and a clear creamy complexion. Her eyes were perhaps her best feature with their heavy fringe of dark lashes and well defined brows. She took after her mother and had always taken her looks for granted, being neither proud nor ashamed of them. Now, suddenly she wondered if there was anything she could do to improve them. She lifted the heavy curtain of hair back from her face and turned this way and that, studying the effect and starting with alarm when a sudden thump on the door shattered her reverie. 'Come out of there,' O'Rourke shouted. 'If we don't leave right away I'll be taking those fashion shots in the dark!'

Hurriedly she bundled her comb and lipstick back into her bag and opened the door to find him already halfway down the stairs. As they climbed into the car she suddenly remembered something.

'Oh—what about the proofs? Have you got them?'

He shook his head, frowning at her as he revved up and slipped the Bentley into gear. 'Of course I haven't. You'll have to come back with me afterwards to get them. They take a couple of hours to dry.'

Watching O'Rourke take the photographs for the fashion feature was fascinating to Cara. The dresses were from a designer collection—mostly evening wear. Taken in the dusky half-light with the natural romantically leafy background of the gardens and employing all the subtle tricks of angle and lighting that had made him one of the top photographers in the business, O'Rourke used all his charm to get the best out of the models; commanding and flirting with them by turns and making instinctively well-timed remarks to get just the facial expression he wanted at the crucial moment. As she watched an elegant, reed-slim creature in floating, ethereal white who, a moment before had been complaining bitterly about the cold, respond to his coaxing like a pet kitten, Cara realised that in his profession it was necessary to be something of a psychologist as well as a wizard with a camera.

During the session the soft breeze that had been blowing all day had strengthened. It hadn't bothered O'Rourke, serving as an extra free aid to his art; making the delicate fabrics and the models' hair behave in the most interesting and dramatic way. But with the freshening wind the temperature had lowered and the girls began to shiver in their flimsy dresses. As the last shot was being taken the rain began to come down in earnest and a sudden clap of thunder overhead made several of the girls scream with alarm.

'All right. Session over. Thanks everyone!' He called resignedly, beginning to put away his gear as the girls scuttled off to change out of their dresses in the tent provided by the designer house.

Cara emerged from where she had been watching. She hugged herself, shivering with the cold and from standing still for so long.

'Thanks for letting me watch. It was fascinating.'

O'Rourke looked up in surprise as though he had forgotten she was there. 'Oh—enjoy it, did you?' He glanced at the sky, then back at her light skirt and jacket. 'You're going to get wet. Didn't you bring a mac or anything?'

'No. I didn't know I was coming, did I?' She pulled up the collar of her jacket against the rain, which by now was beginning to soak through the thin material. O'Rourke shrugged into his leather jacket and zipped it up, then, as another clap of thunder followed a vicious flash of lightning, he thrust a box of equipment into her arms.

'Come on then. Better move quickly. It's quite a way to the car.'

By the time they reached the Bentley, Cara's hair was hanging in wet strands about her face and she was shivering. She climbed into the car and slammed the door angrily. He might have offered her his jacket!

'You'd better take me straight home! I'm soaked.' She glanced at his profile.

He started the car, revving noisily. 'Don't be an idiot. My place is nearer. Besides, you want those proofs, don't you?'

Damn those proofs! 'Well, yes but . . .'

'You can dry out there and warm up with a coffee.' O'Rourke slipped the car into gear and they moved forward.

She sat back resignedly, feeling too cold and bedraggled to argue.

At the flat O'Rourke took the stairs two at a time, pausing to throw his case of equipment into a cupboard. He unzipped his jacket, shaking himself like a wet dog while Cara stood watching uncertainly. He looked at her and nodded towards the door.

'Go on—you know where the bathroom is. I'd take a shower if I were you. You look half frozen.'

In the bathroom she was a little disconcerted to find that there was no lock on the door. However, she peeled off her wet clothes and stepped into the shower, drawing the curtain and turning on the taps. The hot needles of water were like a caress to her chilled body and she was soon glowing with warmth again. She was just reaching out for a towel when O'Rourke's voice close at hand startled her.

'I've brought you a bath robe,' he said from the other side of the curtain. 'I'll hang it on the door for you. Coffee's ready.'

She dried herself and inspected her clothes. Everything was damp except her bra and panties. She decided to take advantage of O'Rourke's robe and slipped it on over them, wrapping it around herself and tying the belt securely. She draped her damp skirt and shirt over the radiator and surveyed herself in the bathroom mirror for the second time that evening, giving her reflection a rueful smile. Earlier she had been wondering if there was anything she could do to improve her appearance. Nature seemed to have taken over in that direction but as she took in the scrubbed face framed by damp tendrils of hair and the brown towelling robe that was about ten sizes too large she reflected wryly that Mother Nature's sense of humour must be working overtime today!

She found O'Rourke in the kitchen. He had changed into a grey tracksuit and was busy putting cups onto a tray. He turned as she came in and gave a shout of laughter.

'God, no! You look like something the cat dragged in! Still, never mind. It'll keep you warm till your own things are dry.'

Stung, she glared at him. 'There's no lock on your bathroom door. You might have taken the trouble to knock!'

He stared at her. 'I don't believe it! Listen sweetheart. I've lost count of the number of female bodies I've photographed; some of them nude and most of them quite spectacular. There are no surprises left for me!'

'Don't call me sweetheart!' she snapped. 'For your information, I am *not* just another female body. And for me it seems there *are* still a few surprises—some of them obviously unpleasant ones!'

He surveyed her with a frown. 'I didn't know there *were* still girls like you around. You're behaving like something out of a Victorian vicarage!'

She raised her eyebrows. 'I thought you said there were no surprises left for you? Well, you were wrong, weren't you?'

'So it seems! And for *your* information, little Miss Prim—I *did* knock. You didn't answer so I just assumed you couldn't hear above the noise of the shower.'

Her face dropped. 'Oh . . .'

For a moment they stared at each other, then his lips began to twitch and he burst into his big, full throated laugh, the sound echoing off the tiled walls until she couldn't help joining in, slightly self-consciously. At last he stopped, putting his hands on her shoulders and looking down into her eyes.

'You're not really angry with me for coming into the bathroom, are you?'

She shook her head, colouring slightly. 'If you really knew the first thing about women, O'Rourke, you'd know that no girl likes being described as "something the cat dragged in."'

The blue eyes were contrite. 'Ah—so that was it! Sorry, Cara.' He dropped a kiss on her forehead, then began to slide his arms around her. 'All I can say is that it must have been a cat of excellent taste and breeding. Actually, you look quite delicious with your face all shiny and your hair wet.' His face began to close in on hers, but she slipped out of his arms and picked up the tray.

'Coffee's getting cold,' she said brightly over her shoulder as she carried it through to the living room.

O'Rourke had made sandwiches to go with the coffee. Doorstep-thick and filled with ham and tomato, they were good and satisfying. Cara tucked into them enthusiastically, sitting on a huge floor cushion in front of the electric fire. She was unaware of O'Rourke's eyes on her until he suddenly said quietly: 'Tell me about yourself, Cara.'

She looked up at him, brushing crumbs from the front of the borrowed robe. 'You know about me. I'm features editor on "Zena" magazine. I like my job and I try to be good at it. I'd like to be an editor one day, or maybe work on one of the big national dailies. I like working with people . . .'

He stopped her with a shake of his head. 'Not things like that. About you—Cara—the person.'

She put her plate on the coffee table and took a sip of her coffee, partly to give herself time to think and partly to hide her face. 'It's all very mundane and boring. My parents parted before I was born, so my mother brought me up alone. Later, I went to a boarding school so that she could work to give

58

us a good standard of living.'

His eyes twinkled at her. 'I take it the school was a convent?'

Her cheeks coloured at the implication. 'It wasn't as a matter of fact.'

'What does your mother do?' he asked.

'She began on the stage, but later took up journalism,' she told him. 'She re-married fairly recently and went to live in France.'

'I see. So now you're all alone.'

'That's right.'

'What does your father do? Do you keep in touch?'

Cara shifted uncomfortably. Why did he want to know so much about her? Questions of this kind always made her uncomfortable. Putting her cup down and making as though to rise, she asked: 'What is this, the third degree?'

He reached out a hand to her shoulder, pressing her back. 'No need to get touchy. I'm sorry. I didn't mean to pry. You don't have to tell me anything if you don't want to.'

'Oh, thanks a lot!' Cara remained on her cushion, feeling trapped and very much aware of the large firm hand, heavy on her shoulder. 'I've nothing to hide. My father works in a bank if you must know and no, we don't keep in touch.' Her cheeks flushed crimson. She had no idea why she'd said it. The lie had slipped out as glibly as though she told it every day. O'Rourke accepted it.

'I understand why you're so much on the defensive now,' he told her. 'It may surprise you to know that we have a lot in common; though your upbringing sounds rather more upmarket than mine.'

'Oh?' She looked up at him, her expressive eyes betraying her interest.

He nodded. 'My parents split up too. My mother walked out when I was eight. We lived in a Dublin back street and my father worked in a factory. I daresay she found it all too much like drudgery. My father devoted the rest of his life to bringing me up—sacrificed all his free time and every penny he earned to give me the best education he could. Everything I am today I owe to him.'

Cara felt a little ashamed of her defensive attitude and asked: 'Is that why you have such a poor opinion of women in general?'

He took a handful of her hair and pulled her head back so that he could look into her eyes. 'And who said I have a poor opinion of women?' he demanded. 'I depend on them for my work most of the time, don't I?'

'That doesn't mean you have to respect them.' Wincing, she tried to squirm out of his grasp. 'The way you're acting now isn't exactly chivalrous, is it?'

He bent and kissed her swiftly. 'Perhaps that's more convincing,' he said softly. He lowered himself onto the floor beside her. The hand that had grasped her hair relaxed and

60

began to caress the back of her neck and her heart began to quicken with a mixture of alarm and excitement. She told herself that she could leave right now if she wanted to, but she knew instinctively that, were she to move, the hand on her neck would tighten.

With his other hand he cradled her face and kissed her again, this time unhurriedly, his lips tender at first, then searching and sensual, finally demanding as his mouth hardened, forcing her lips to part for him. His hand slid slowly down her spine, pressing her close so that she could feel the hardness of his muscular body, while the other hand insinuated itself inside the robe at the waist, drawing from her an involuntary gasp as it made contact with her bare skin. She felt his fingers slide tantalisingly upwards over her ribs, stopping when they encountered the silk and lace of her bra. Once more she felt helpless—as she had when he kissed her yesterday—it was almost as though his kiss acted as a kind of drug, reducing her to a weak, defenceless state. When he swiftly and expertly disposed of the flimsy bra and cradled one breast she was shocked to find her nipple tautening sensitively to his touch. Very gently he began to lower her to the floor, his mouth once more on hers. Suddenly panic gave her back her strength and she pressed both hands against his chest.

'No!'

He let her go, looking at her in mild surprise. 'What is it?'

In her mind she grasped at the first thought that came into her head. 'The proofs,' she said. 'I—we—forgot the proofs.'

He laughed and pulled her to him again. 'They won't come to any harm. You can have them in the morning.'

She gave him a violent push and rolled away, scrambling unceremoniously to her feet to glare down at him, her face hot with indignation.

'The *morning*! What do you mean? You surely don't expect me to stay the night with you? Just what do you take me for, O'Rourke?'

He sat on the floor, smiling unrepentantly up at her. 'I take you for what you are—a lovely and desirable girl, who made a bargain with me,' he told her calmly.

Her heart hammered wildly against her ribs. Did he really believe what he was saying? 'All the opinions I'd formed about you are right,' she snapped, wrapping the robe around herself as though it were a suit of armour. 'Except that you're even more sexist than I thought.'

He gave her his slow, insolent smile. 'None of that seemed to be bothering you just now. Be honest with yourself at least, Cara. I think I can tell when a girl's attracted to me.'

Furious, she strode to the door, pausing when she reached it. 'You're not even my *type*,' she flung over her shoulder. 'I *loathe* beards for a start. In my opinion they're just for men like you to hide behind! I'm going to get dressed now. I'd be grateful if you'd telephone for a taxi for me.'

To her surprise he did exactly as she asked. When she emerged from the bathroom in her rain-crumpled clothes he was in the kitchen with his back towards her, whistling unconcernedly as he washed the cups. He told her coolly over his shoulder that her taxi was waiting in the mews. It was only when she had reached her own flat and went to pay the driver that she discovered the envelope containing the proofs tucked inside her handbag. With them was a note. It read: *'Sexist, I may be, but at least I kept my side of the bargain!'*

CHAPTER FOUR

When Cara handed the proofs of the photographs for the Janet Lorimar feature to her editor the following morning, Anita was delighted and impressed. Even more so when she saw that Cara had also produced the first draft of the accompanying article. She looked up at her over the tops of her spectacles.

'Well done! How did you manage to get O'Rourke to re-do the photographs so quickly? Did you take my advice and flatter the man's ego a little?'

Cara coloured. 'Not as much as he would have liked, I suspect. That man really is the most sexist—the most conceited ...' She stopped herself, biting her lip as she noticed Anita's amused expression.

'Endurance above and beyond the call of duty, eh?' she said with a smile. 'Anyway, the results are excellent. You must have worked very hard. I shall take you out to lunch today to celebrate. We still haven't had that talk.' She looked again at the photographs and then back at Cara. 'I'll leave you to make your own final selection of these, then you can telephone and tell him to go ahead whenever you like.'

Cara hesitated. 'Oh—I thought you might want to do that yourself.'

Anita looked up in surprise. 'No need for that. Besides, you know him better than I do now.'

Cara smiled grimly to herself at the irony of the remark as she went back to her office. Overnight she had been doing a lot of thinking. Unable to sleep she had got up and worked on the Janet Lorimar article, which accounted for the draft which now lay on Anita's desk. Remarks O'Rourke had made earlier had come flooding back as she lay in the darkness, disturbing her mind and angering her too much for sleep. *What's it worth?—I didn't get where I am today by doing*

64

favours for people.' Obviously he had been under the impression that she had made a bargain with him—and that she had welshed on her side of it.

Behind her closed eyelids his vibrant image was indelibly printed. She saw him at work, his strong, handsome face a mask of concentration as he planned his shots and coaxed the models. He had stripped off his jacket to work and Cara saw again in her mind's eye, the firm tanned arms with their covering of dark hair and the smooth movement of the strong shoulder muscles under the thin cotton tee-shirt. Angrily she had turned over and punched her pillow as she tried to blot out the memory of his kiss—the sheer masculine assertiveness of him and the way he had taken it for granted that she would go to bed with him in return for rushing through the proofs. Although she didn't admit it to herself, his calm acceptance of her refusal was perhaps the most wounding memory of all. Obviously O'Rourke was used to getting what he wanted. What had he said? *'I don't allow people to use me—however attractive they happen to be!'* 'Women are like buses to O'Rourke,' she told the ceiling. 'Lose one and it doesn't matter. There'd always be another along soon! How dare he treat me like all the rest?' But a deeply disturbing small voice insisted on asking: 'Why not? What's so special about you?'

That was when she finally gave up on trying to sleep and got up to work on the article. But as soon as she began thinking of Janet, her train of thought directed her towards the T.V. play she had accidentally stumbled on and that thought led logically to Clive.

Poor Clive. He was beginning to go through a traumatic time—what is known as a 'midlife crisis', except for him it was far more traumatic than for anyone else. When one was renowned for one's dashing looks and personality it must be hard to come to terms with their gradual decline; like those sad child stars whose public couldn't accept their growing up.

The best thing for Clive to do would be to take a new direction; to take his courage and his talent in both hands and show the world what a good actor he was; wipe out the playboy image. It could mean the start of a whole new phase in his life and Janet's play might be just the part to launch him on it. She made up her mind to go and see him about it. Somehow she must arrange for him to meet the novelist and discuss it. But finding a discreet way of bringing about a meeting between the two of them without declaring her own personal interest wouldn't be easy; especially as she was sworn to secrecy over the existence of the play. Maybe one way to pave the way would be to make the article on Janet as good as she possibly could.

She had reapplied herself to the work with

renewed enthusiasm, grateful for something positive to do to take her mind off the discomforting images of O'Rourke that haunted her. She finished just as dawn was breaking with an agonising ache in her neck and shoulders, but a small spark of hope in her heart.

Back in her office she spread the proofs before her and studied them carefully. They really were good. She had been too angry to look at them properly last night. It was going to be difficult making her choice. The spread would take four. A portrait of Janet and three smaller ones of her at work. She chose the portrait first, a lovely one of the author in her study, a shelf of her six bestsellers in the background. Cara looked at it, wondering if Anita would consider making it the cover picture for that issue. The sudden thought that it would bring O'Rourke another royalty fee and a special credit almost made her change her mind. Why go out of the way to boost that man's already inflated ego? All the same ... She picked up the portrait and looked at it again. It certainly would make a good cover— plus a boost for her own article. It would please Janet too and perhaps indirectly, help Clive. Oh well, if she remembered she might mention it to Anita at lunch.

When she had finally chosen the four she took a deep breath and picked up the telephone, asking for an outside line. Better do this one by herself. She didn't want to risk anyone in the office overhearing the conversation in case O'Rourke made any reference to last night. The telephone rang twice then there was a click and—

'Hello there. Corin O'Rourke here. Sorry, I'm out at the moment, but if you'd like to leave a message or number I'll get back to you as soon as I can.'

The voice with its lilting hint of Irish brogue oozed charm and Cara ground her teeth with irritation. Stupid! She might have known he would be out at this time of the morning. Fighting down a feeling of anti-climax, she gave the numbers of the photographs she wanted for the article in a very brisk and business-like tone, adding: 'My editor would be grateful if you could let us have the work as soon as you can, please.' As she put down the receiver she was annoyed to find that her hand was shaking.

The rest of the morning went well. Anita sent Jennifer through to say she had read the draft and approved it. When it was typed, Cara took it, along with the proofs, to the art department to talk to Jim Marshall, the art editor. It was lunchtime before she knew it.

Jennifer had booked them a table at Mario's, the little Italian restaurant close to the office block. It was where Anita usually took her freelance writers. She was well known there and the waiters always saw to it that she wasn't kept waiting. They settled themselves comfortably in their corner booth and Anita ordered a dry Martini each, grinning across at Cara.

'I think we deserve this, especially you. You must have been up half the night, working on that article. No wonder you're looking so peaky. Maybe a good lunch will put the roses back into your cheeks.' As they sipped their drinks she glanced at Cara.

'Have you heard from your mother lately?' she asked out of the blue.

Cara looked up in surprise. 'Yes, I had a letter the other day. She seems very happy— loves her new life in Paris—and her new husband, of course.'

Anita paused, twisting the stem of her glass. 'You don't—resent him, do you, Cara?' she asked.

Cara laughed. 'Why should I? If you mean do I feel he's taken my mother out of the country and out of reach, no. We were never all that close. I'm glad she's happy.'

'Good. She must have been bitter about men after her first marriage. You told me once that it broke up before you were even born.'

Cara shrugged. 'It took her a long time to trust one again, but I don't think she was actually bitter.' She wondered what all this was leading up to. Glancing up at Anita she waited for the next question.

'And you?' Anita asked. 'How do you feel

about men—after your own father deserting you, I mean? That must have clouded your view of the opposite sex somewhat.'

'He didn't desert *me*,' Cara said a little too quickly. 'He didn't know of my existence unti—' She bit her lip and began again: 'My mother didn't know that she was pregnant when they parted. When she did find out she decided to keep it to herself.'

'I see.' Anita looked at her. 'Haven't you ever been curious about him?' she asked.

Cara shrugged. 'Maybe, but what's done is done. I have my own life to lead.' She finished her drink and decided to ask what was in her mind. 'Anita—what are you trying to say? Are you unhappy about my work?'

The other woman shook her head firmly. 'Far from it. It's just that I like to know a little about what goes on in the heads of my staff. I'd like you to feel you could confide in me— come to me with your problems—specially now that your mother isn't around.'

But Cara wasn't fooled. 'Come on. What did I do? I'd rather you were straight with me.'

Anita started to speak but at that moment the waiter brought their soup and she had to wait until he had gone before she made a fresh start.

'I like the people who work with me to be happy. Sometimes you seem a bit abrasive—a little too guarded with your male colleagues. They notice it, you know. In spite of what you

70

think, men aren't always what they seem on the surface. Some of them are quite sensitive creatures. Then there's your attitude towards your job. Sometimes I have the feeling that you rely on it too much. Dedication is one thing, but there's a saying . . .'

'All work and no play?' Cara suggested.

The editor smiled. 'Exactly. I'd like to see you going out and enjoying yourself more— sporting a string of boyfriends like the girls in the typing pool.' She grinned ruefully. 'Well, maybe not quite that, but you know what I mean. Don't take life so seriously. It's all too short.'

O'Rourke's words echoed unbidden through her head: *'Life's a ball if you let it be.'* Then there was Clive's: *'You should go out and enjoy yourself more.'*

'You're not the first to make that kind of observation,' she admitted. 'But surely, if I get my kicks from working hard where's the harm? It seems to me that the true-love syndrome is a myth, used to promote cosmetics and boxes of chocolates.'

'What a cynical view for a young girl to hold!' Anita's eyebrows arched. 'Anyway, you don't have to be *in love* with a man to enjoy his company, you know,' she pointed out. 'That's what I meant about you being too serious.' She shrugged. 'Still, if that's all it is, fair enough. I was just worried that you might have some kind of hang-up about men. Because of your background.'

Cara laughed. 'I've never given that much thought to it. I can take them or leave them. I suppose I do have quite high standards—ideals, I suppose you'd call them. I haven't yet met a man who comes anywhere near them.'

'Well, be careful. In my experience women with high ideals about men usually end up falling for the worst kind of rogue!' And with this profound remark the subject closed. Over coffee Anita said casually: 'Oh, by the way, talking of going out and enjoying yourself, I had a call from Smithson and Browne's this morning. They're throwing a launch party for Janet Lorimar's book and they wanted to know whom they should invite from the magazine—the names of all those involved with the feature we're doing.'

Cara looked up. 'Oh, that's kind of them.'

'Yes. I gave yours of course, and Jim Marshall's. His graphics are very good and I thought he'd like to go.'

'When is it?'

'Week after next,' Anita told her. 'The book doesn't come out for another month, but by then Janet will have left for the States on a promotion tour. She's recording her T.V. appearances in advance too.'

Cara made a mental note of this piece of information. If she wanted to see Janet and broach the subject of the T.V. play she would have to be quick off the mark.

'It occurred to me that O'Rourke's portrait of her would make a good cover picture,' she said. 'And by the way, I expect you'll want her to look the article over in case there's anything she wants to retract.'

'That's a point. And of course her publishers will want to vet it too.' Anita looked at her. 'In view of her tight schedule you'd better see her as soon as possible. Give her a ring when we get back to the office. As for the cover picture, I'd had the same thought myself.' She looked at her watch. 'Heavens! look at the time. I have an appointment at half-past two. Jennifer will be biting her fingernails to the elbows, thinking I've forgotten!'

On the short walk back to the office she touched Cara's arm. 'Remember what I said. Try to take a more relaxed view of life. Laugh more. Try to see a lighter side to life.'

Back at her desk, Cara sat for a while, thinking about the lunchtime conversation. Maybe Anita was right; maybe O'Rourke's casual view of life and relationships was best. She sighed, knowing that she simply wasn't made like that. She bruised too easily. The kind of quick affair he had in mind just wasn't her scene. Instinctively she knew it would only end in her being hurt and that was something she wasn't prepared to risk—certainly not for a man like O'Rourke!

She telephoned Janet and got her

73

housekeeper who told her that Miss Lorimar was busy but would see her at four if she cared to drop in. Cara said she would and rang off to apply herself to the work that had been piling up over the last two days.

At four o'clock the door of Janet Lorimar's apartment was opened by Mrs Phillips, the middle-aged housekeeper.

'Ah yes. You'll be from the magazine,' she said when Cara told her her name. 'Miss Lorimar asked me to show you through to the patio. She's having tea. Would you like some?'

Cara smiled. 'That would be very nice.'

The housekeeper nodded. 'I'll bring another cup. Please go through. I think you know the way.'

Cara opened the door of the elegant drawing room, then stopped on the threshold, the breath catching in her throat. On the floor was a familiar-looking leather briefcase; on the coffee table sat a camera, while a black leather jacket was draped carelessly over the arm of one chair.

Her first instinct was to turn and run, but before she could move Janet's voice called:

'We're out here, having tea. Do join us, my dear.'

Her mouth dry, Cara went towards the open glass doors. On the patio Janet sat at a white wrought-iron table, dispensing tea. O'Rourke sat with his back to her. He was wearing his customary working clothes, jeans and a white tee-shirt which clung to his body like a second skin, emphasising his superb physique. He didn't bother to turn and look at Cara as she stood uncertainly in the doorway but Janet rose and came towards her, hand outstretched.

'Do come and have some tea, Cara. Corin has been taking a new portrait of me for the book jacket and the publicity tour. My publishers suddenly decided that the old one was out of date.' She smiled impishly. 'I'm afraid they were rather cross with me for changing my hair colour since the original one was taken. But it isn't always we women who like to change the way we look, is it?' She took Cara's hand and led her out to the table, pulling out one of the elegant little wrought-iron chairs. 'There, talk to Corin while I go and ask Mrs Phillips to make us a fresh pot.'

Cara made herself look at O'Rourke for the first time. Then she gasped with shock. For one confused second she thought she must have made a mistake—that the back turned towards her hadn't belonged to O'Rourke after all. The man at the table was *clean-shaven*. For the first time she could see the strong, hard line of his jaw, the square chin with its slight cleft and the smooth hollows and planes of his cheek bones. His hair had been cut too. Shorter, it lay in crisp layers, winging back from his temples, the sunlight burnishing its rich chestnut colour. Now she understood Janet's remark about women not being alone

75

in the need for change. The sound of O'Rourke clearing his throat brought her to earth.

'Excuse me for drawing attention to it, but your mouth is open!'

She closed it and sat down abruptly. 'I hardly—you've had your hair cut and—and your beard shaved off,' she said superfluously.

His mouth twisted cynically. 'You noticed. How observant!'

'But—why?'

He slapped his forehead with the flat of one palm. 'God in heaven! I'll never understand women! Didn't you tell me yourself last night that you loathed beards?'

She stared at him. 'You're not trying to tell me you did it because of what *I* said?'

He shook his head indignantly. 'No, I'm not!'

Janet came back with the freshly brewed tea and a cup for Cara, who opened her briefcase and handed her a copy of the article.

'If you wouldn't mind just looking this through while I'm here we could go ahead with it,' she explained.

The novelist peered at it. 'I need my reading glasses. Look, I'll go through to the study and read it. You two help yourselves to sandwiches and cake—whatever you want, and entertain each other for a moment, will you?' She rose, taking her cup and the article with her.

When she had gone there was an awkward

silence. Cara sipped her tea and helped herself to a wafer-thin cucumber sandwich. Why on earth had she said that about his shaving off his beard on her account? She glanced across at O'Rourke. He was sitting with one leg crooked across the other, leafing through a glossy magazine. He certainly looked more relaxed than she felt! She pushed the plate towards him. 'Want one of these?' He shook his head without looking up. She cleared her throat, then said: 'While I think of it, my editor is hoping to use your portrait of Janet for the cover, if you've no objections.' Remembering Anita's words of advice about the delicate male ego, she added: 'It was my idea actually.'

He nodded absently without taking his eyes off the magazine. So much for trying to soothe the savage breast! She wished she hadn't bothered. There was a small silence before curiosity got the better of her and she asked: 'Why *did* you do it—shave off your beard, I mean?'

He closed the magazine and stretched out his long legs, looking at her for a long moment, one dark eyebrow raised. 'You heard what Janet said. Men like a change of image too. And I must say I've quite enjoyed all the double-takes I've received today.' He leaned across the table, his arms folded. 'And just to put the record straight, Cara, it had *nothing* to do with anything you might have said.'

'Oh—no, well, I just thought . . .' She trailed

77

off, colouring as he studied her face with embarrasing candour.

'Tell me something,' he interrupted insistently. 'Every time you get yourself a new hair-do or decide to wear a daring new fashion, is it because of a chance remark some guy makes to you?'

She blushed. 'No, of course not.'

He nodded. 'Of course not!' he repeated mockingly. He rose from the table and looked down at her, his blue eyes suddenly flinty. 'Your attempt at making amends for what happened last night is pathetically transparent, Cara. Do you really think that having one of my portraits on the cover of your mediocre little magazine means anything to me? Forget about last night. You got what you wanted and made an exit worthy of a tragedy queen! All in all, you should be congratulating yourself!' He walked into the drawing room and picked up his jacket, coming back with it hooked over his shoulder by one finger.

'I'll make a prediction though, Cara.' He stood looking down at her, the blue eyes glinting dangerously. 'You'll be back! Make no mistake about it. But next time, it'll be *your* choice—and you'll *ask* to stay!'

She felt the blood sting her cheeks as she stared up into those blue eyes, momentarily speechless. There were so many things she wanted to say that the words stuck in her throat. But the half of her mind that stood

78

detachedly aside, observing, registered that in spite of the removal of his beard, he *still* looked like a pirate.

'You have to be joking!' she countered, gathering herself at last. 'I'd die first. As for my trying to make amends, that's utter rubbish. As far as I'm aware, I've nothing to make amends for. It's *you* who should be doing that! You must be a very bad judge of character if you believe I'd ever make the sort of bargain you were expecting! As for my ever coming to your studio again of my own choice—there is *no way* that could ever happen!'

He looked at her for a moment, eyes narrowed. 'For someone so innocent you're very much on the defensive.'

She stared at him speechlessly, spluttering slightly as she feverishly tried to find the words to tell him how wrong he was. But before she could frame them he turned abruptly.

'I've got to go. Tell Janet I'll ring her. 'Bye.'

When Janet came back she was still trembling and when the author handed her back the folded typescript, a smile on her face, Cara stared blankly up at her, almost forgetting her real reason for being here.

'Don't change a thing. I think it's very good,' Janet glanced round. 'Oh—has Corin gone?'

Cara pulled herself together. 'Oh—yes, he asked me to say goodbye for him. I think he had a pressing engagement.'

'Ah, I see. Well, never mind.' Janet sat down and took one of the cucumber sandwiches. 'What did you think of his new look?'

'Sorry?'

'The new, clean "All American Regular Guy" image.' She laughed. 'I really can't think what got into him. I'm all for change. It's just that it seems to have done so little for him. I've never known him so bad tempered.'

'Really?' Cara asked weakly.

'Yes. He was quite snappy with me when I talked while he was photographing me. Quite unlike himself. And now, rushing off like that . . .' She looked at Cara. 'Still, enough about bad tempered men. We should thank our lucky stars that neither of us has to bother with their wretched moods! I hope you're coming to my launch party.'

'Yes—thank you.' Cara was desperately trying to put O'Rourke out of her mind. His black mood had thrown her off balance, making her forget all the things she had planned to say to Janet. On the way to the apartment she had been racking her brain to think of a suitably casual way to bring up the subject of the T.V. play and now she made a conscious effort to force her mind back onto that track.

'Are you working on anything new at the moment?' she asked at last. She didn't want to appear to probe about the play in case Janet might suspect her of planning to break her promise to keep it secret.

The author shook her head. 'I'm having a rest until my tour begins. Though of course I'm hoping my new piece of work will take wing soon. If it does I may have some revising to do, so I want to keep my mind clear for that.' She leaned forward confidentially. 'By the way, my dear, thank you very much for the suggestion you made. I thought about it a lot after you'd gone and you know, you're quite right. Clive Redway would be perfect for the part, if only someone could persuade him to do it.'

Cara felt her heart quicken with excitement. 'Well—I don't know, of course—but maybe his agent . . .' she said haltingly.

'He has already been contacted,' Janet told her confidentially. 'I called my ex-husband this morning and we had a long discussion about casting. He said he would get in touch.' Her face dropped slightly. 'He also told me not to build up my hopes though. Said he knows Clive personally and couldn't see him agreeing to anything that diminished his glamour image.'

'I—*might* be able to help,' Cara said, holding her breath.

Janet stared at her. 'You mean you *know* him?'

'I—have contacts.'

'Well, obviously I'd be grateful for anything you could do,' Janet told her. 'Getting an actor of Clive Redway's calibre to star in my first T.V. play would obviously be an enormous help.'

'I promise I'll see what I can do.' Cara got to her feet, aware that it was time to leave. If she stayed here much longer she might let slip more information than she intended. 'I'm so glad you're pleased with the article. And thanks for the invitation. I'll see you at the party.'

She was waiting for the lift when she heard someone call her name and turned to see Mrs Phillips hurrying towards her. The housekeeper was out of breath as she tried to speak.

'Oh, thank goodness. I didn't want to interrupt you while you were in conference with Miss Lorimar.' She held out a small leather case. 'Mr O'Rourke telephoned about fifteen minutes ago. He said he thought he'd left this behind. I think it's called a light meter or something. He said he needed it urgently. Miss Lorimar said you'd probably be seeing him before we would.'

Cara's eyes opened wide. 'Oh! Well . . .' At that moment the lift arrived and the doors opened to receive her. Before she could say another word Mrs Phillips pushed the case into her hand.

'Thank you *so* much, Miss Dean. Chelsea is right out of my way. It would have taken me hours taking it to his studio after work, what with the rush hour and everything.'

As the lift smoothly descended, Cara looked at the case in her hand, wondering what to do. It was out of *her* way too. She looked at her watch and made up her mind. She'd do a detour and go there with it now. She had no wish to make a double journey in the rush hour. Besides, this way she could deliver it while O'Rourke was still out of the way. She could leave the instrument with a neighbour— if it wasn't small enough to push through his letter box.

It was a warm afternoon and by the time she arrived at Jay's Mews she was hot and wilting like the dusty geraniums in their window boxes. The little cobbled street was empty. No sign of the Bentley. She heaved a sigh of relief. She had made the right decision.

Unzipping her briefcase she drew out the light meter in its case and tried to push it through the letter box. It was just a fraction too large and stuck halfway. It was then that she discovered that the front door was open. As she pushed, it clicked and swung back on its hinges.

For a moment she stood there, uncertain what to do. Clearly O'Rourke had failed to pull the door to behind him properly when he went out. She would take the light meter up to the studio, then leave, making sure that the door was securely locked this time.

As she made her way up the stairs she shook

her head. The man must be stupid. He must have thousands of pounds worth of photographic equipment in the studio, yet he could be so careless over locking up!

At the top of the stairs she stood looking around. Today the place looked unusually tidy. Maybe this was his cleaning lady's day to clean up. She walked across the room and drew aside the curtains that divided the living room from the studio, slipping inside. She would leave the light meter here—maybe scribble a note and . . .

'Well, well! If it isn't the celebrated Miss Dean!'

The voice made her spin round, uttering a sharp little cry of alarm. O'Rourke was standing in the doorway of his small darkroom, drying his hands on a towel and looking at her coolly, a devil glinting in his eyes.

'Well now, who'd have though my prediction would have come true this soon? And after all your denials that wild horses wouldn't get you back inside my lair!'

CHAPTER FIVE

Cara stared at O'Rourke, utterly speechless. To be caught like this! It was infuriating. Her face rigid, she held out the light meter in its case.

84

'I—I brought this. You telephoned to say you'd left it behind ...' Suddenly a suspicion crept into her mind. 'You did it deliberately!' She took a step towards him. 'You *did*, didn't you? Just so that you could prove a point!'

'Do you really believe I'd resort to a trick like that?' He held up his hand. 'No! Don't answer that.' He threw down the towel he had been drying his hands on and took the light meter from her trembling hands. 'Think about it,' he said. 'For all I knew you'd already left when I rang. I thought Janet might send Mrs Phillips round with it, or put it into a taxi. I really didn't care as long as I got it back quickly.'

Cara looked at him disbelievingly. 'I don't believe you. You must have several of those things.'

O'Rourke caressed the leather case lovingly. 'Ah, but not like this one. All artists have their favourite pieces of equipment, you know; artists have their favourite brushes, sculptors have pet chisels. It's almost a superstition. With me, it's this.'

Shrugging, she turned towards the door. 'Well, you've got it back now. I'd better be getting back to the office.'

His hand shot out to grab her arm. 'Cara— don't go. Not for a moment. Look, I am pleased to get this back—and that it was you who brought it. It gives me a chance to apologise for this afternoon. I've been in a foul

85

mood all day. I even snapped at poor sweet Janet.'

'That's quite all right. I never gave it another thought.' She preferred him in a bad temper. At least she could snap back. Contrition was something else. She edged towards the door. Already she could feel her senses reacting traitorously to the pressure of his hand on her arm. It made her uneasy. 'I really do have to get back to the office,' she told him breathlessly. 'The feature on Janet Lorimar has taken up all my time over the past few days and the work is piling up alarmingly. I was hoping to . . .'

'Let me give you dinner this evening then—by way of an apology?'

He stopped her words in mid-flow—her breath too. She stared up at him, her eyes wide. 'Oh! There's no need, really—I . . .'

He moved almost imperceptibly closer. 'Cara, you'd better say yes.' His voice was soft and his breath caressed her cheek. 'Because I'm not going to let you go until you do. And if you make me stand here like this much longer I'm going to . . .'

'All right,' she said, tearing her gaze away from his. 'All right—but I shall have to work late to catch up. I can't possibly make it till nine o'clock.'

She didn't wait to hear his reply—or to look again into the hypnotic deep blue of his eyes. Her feet thudded down the stairs in unison with her heart. At the bottom she let herself out, slamming the door behind her. As she hurried along the cobbled street she thought she could feel those compelling blue eyes boring into her back and she pictured him watching her retreat from the studio window. But she didn't dare look up to see if he was really there.

*   *   *

In the lift as she left the office that evening Jennifer looked at her speculatively.

'Got a date?'

Cara looked at her in surprise. 'Yes, as a matter of fact. How did you guess?'

The other girl grinned. 'Intuition. Something about the look of you. You've got a sort of sparkle—colour in your cheeks too.'

'That's probably panic!' Cara held out her heavily loaded briefcase. 'Because I'm wondering how on earth I'm going to catch up with all this work before nine o'clock on Monday morning and still go out to dinner tonight as well.'

Jennifer grinned. 'A heavy date, eh? One who can't be put off?'

'One who *won't* be put off!' Cara said.

'Ah, the persistent kind. The plot thickens!' Jennifer grinned gleefully.

The lift came to a halt with its customary little jolt and Cara stepped out with some relief. Calling goodnight to Jennifer she made a bolt for the nearest underground station, glad to escape from the secretary's probing questions. The sooner she could get home and start work, the better!

It was eight-fifteen when she finally put the cover on her portable typewriter. Leaning back in her chair she stretched her arms above her head, easing the tension from her neck and shoulders; wishing she could make herself a sandwich and a cup of coffee and climb into bed with her transistor radio for company. But O'Rourke would be here in forty-five minutes, by which time she must be ready to go out to dinner. She sighed and rose to wander into the bedroom and open the wardrobe. What could she wear? She finally narrowed the choice down to two—a coral and white flowered silk—very suitable for a warm spring evening; or a sophisticated black velvet suit with coffee accessories. Her first instinct was to choose the latter, knowing it would make her feel more confident. But, remembering Anita's advice she put it firmly back on its rail and laid out the more frivolous flowered silk instead. After a quick shower she made up her face carefully and arranged her hair casually, letting it tumble about her shoulders.

Although she had been ready for the past fifteen minutes, Cara started violently when the bell rang at ten past nine, jumping to her feet. For a moment she forced herself to stay where she was, fighting down the impulse to run to the door. Really! She was behaving like a teenager on her first date. After a suitable delay she walked slowly to the door, trying to calm the dull thud of her heartbeat as she went; telling herself how foolish she was. She reached out her hand to the door handle, taking a deep breath before turning it. This was ridiculous, she told herself. She didn't even particularly want to go out with the man, so why should she react like this?

When she opened the door his eyes swept over her with the usual frank appraisal. Without waiting to be asked, he walked inside, filling her tiny hallway with his broad shoulders and his strong personality. He began by apologising for being late.

Cara looked casually at her watch. 'Are you? I really hadn't noticed. I've been working flat out ever since I got home. If you hadn't been late I probably wouldn't have been ready.' She squirmed inwardly at the glibness with which the lie tripped off her tongue. It had been madness to agree to see him again. The man really *did* bring out the worst in her! She looked at his well-cut trousers and expensive soft suède jacket and ventured:

'Where are we going?'

'A little Italian *ristorante* I'm rather fond of in Soho,' he told her. 'The owners are friends of mine. If you like Italian food you have a treat in store; if you don't—prepare to be reformed!'

Cara toyed with the idea of telling him she had eaten an Italian lunch, but decided not to bother. She had the distinct impression that it wouldn't have made any difference. 'Oh—good,' she muttered.

Downstairs, the Bentley waited at the kerb like some great predatory monster, impatient to be unleashed. It occurred to Cara that the car and its owner had much in common! She climbed in and glanced at O'Rourke as he started the engine. He really did look different without his beard. The skin of his cheeks was surprisingly smooth, the hard, strong angle of his jaw compensated by the sensuous curve of his mouth. The eyes were slightly hooded, their lids fringed with thick dark lashes and those heavy, expressive brows. He felt her gaze and turned to smile at her. Blushing, she looked away.

'Is it far—this restaurant?' she asked.

'No, why, are you hungry?'

'No—well, yes, I am actually,' she admitted, realising that she hadn't eaten since lunch and that was nine hours ago.

The *Ristorante Roma* was tiny and tucked away down a Soho side street. The owner and his wife, whom O'Rourke greeted enthusiastically as Alfredo and Maria, exclaimed with delight at seeing their friend. For the first few minutes they chattered excitedly to him in Italian and O'Rourke surprised Cara by answering them fluently in their own language. The man was about fifty with a huge girth and a grin to match. His wife Maria was short and plump with quick dark eyes. She was effusive about the change in O'Rourke. Flinging up her hands with a little scream, she cried:

'Cor-*een*-a! *Ma-ma mia!* You shave-a-the face!' Reaching up, she stroked his cheeks admiringly. 'Aaah—*Va benissimo!*' Her black eyes flashed as she laughed suggestively up at him. 'You do this-a for Maria, huh? You always know how I hate-a-the face-fuzz!'

O'Rourke bent and gave her a resounding kiss. 'Of course! Who else would I shave for but the *beautiful* Signora Andretti?'

But Alfredo, who had been sizing Cara up with undisguised approval, exclaimed derisively. '*Huh!* For you? Use-a-your eyes, woman! Our friend, Corin got-a-himself one fine woman!'

All three laughed at Cara's blushes and Alfredo made a great show of finding them a secluded corner booth. Slapping the tablecloth vigorously with a napkin and pulling out Cara's chair for her with a flourish, he grinned across at O'Rourke, informing him in a stage whisper that here they could—'*Hold-a-the hands!*'

The couple fussed over them, keeping their wine glasses full to the brim from the large bottle they insisted was 'on the house' and when Alfredo discovered that her name was

91

Cara he gave a whoop of delight and produced a guitar with which he proceeded to serenade them in true Italian fashion. She found herself almost rigid with embarrassment as his penetrating voice filled the small restaurant and the other diners turned to look at them with curiosity.

'*Cara mia mine ...*' Alfredo sang enthusiastically in a piercingly strangulated tenor, gazing at her soulfully with sloe-dark eyes. O'Rourke passed her the Chianti bottle.

'Have another drink,' he invited lazily, his eyes amused. 'You need at least half a bottle inside you here to numb the English reserve.'

He was right. Cara found that after another two glasses she began to unwind and enjoy herself. Maria's food was delicious. She produced true Italian peasant-style dishes, filling and nourishing and Alfredo's wine was the perfect accompaniment. Coffee, when it came, was hot and strong. Alfredo informed them when he brought it that it was: 'Like-a-the love that follow!' He kissed his fingertips to Cara as he put the tray down before her, giving her a smouldering smile and turning to punch O'Rourke playfully on the shoulder. But by this time Cara's embarrassment was a thing of the past. As she poured the coffee she was suddenly aware that O'Rourke was watching her.

'Have you enjoyed yourself?' he asked.

She laughed. 'Yes, after the initial shock.'

She glanced across the room to where the Italian couple were conducting a noisy, good-natured argument behind the bar. 'They're wonderful, aren't they? They really love people. How did you get to know them?'

'It was when I first came over to England to make my fortune,' he told her. 'They took me on as a waiter, would you believe? It was my "day job". I was a real innocent abroad in those days—didn't know anyone and hadn't a place to stay. They took me under their wing. That first year I lived as one of their family. They were like mother and father to me. I'll never forget their warmth and kindness—or their wonderful food!'

'And did they teach you to speak Italian?' she asked.

He laughed. 'Alfredo and Maria have four sons and at mealtimes everyone talks at once. In those circumstances you learn fast or go hungry!' He looked at her empty cup. 'If you've finished, shall we go?'

She nodded and they rose from the table. O'Rourke picked up the lacy shawl that lay over the back of her chair and draped it over her shoulders, allowing his fingers to brush her neck as he lifted her hair clear. They waved to the Andrettis and O'Rourke called out:

'*Grazie. Siamo stati molto bene! Buona notte!*'

The Italian couple stood behind the bar, nodding and smiling their approval. Alfredo turned to his wife, his eyes melting sentimentally.

'This time for Corin is-a-the *real* thing!' he told her with satisfaction.

Outside darkness had fallen and the street was ablaze with coloured lights and the gaudy display of after-dark Soho. It was some way to where they had parked the car. O'Rourke took her hand as they walked. She didn't try to pull it away. Somehow its warmth and strength were reassuring. As they got into the car he said suddenly:

'I wish you'd call me Corin.'

She looked at him in surprise. 'Oh—all right.'

'We got off on the wrong foot, didn't we?' he said. 'Both said and did things that touched each other on the raw?'

'Did we?'

'You know damned well we did!' There was a touch of impatience in his voice as he turned to look at her. 'I should have known better than to rush you, especially after what you told me about your background.'

She spun round angrily. 'Why does everyone keep harping on about my background? Anyone would think I was some kind of *casualty*!' She looked down at her hands. 'Anyway—I said some nasty things to you too. I admit that I wanted to hit back, so we're quits. I'm sorry.' She turned to look at him. 'We might as well face the fact that we're two totally different kinds of people. Poles apart. It's no wonder we clashed.'

He moved nearer. 'Now that we've accepted that, we could do something about it.'

Her heart began to do odd things as his arm slipped round her shoulders and she felt his strength engulfing her.

'C-could we?' she whispered.

'Oh yes, Cara.' His lips brushed her forehead as his other arm drew her closer. 'Oh yes—we could.' As his lips found hers she seemed to turn to liquid. Closing her eyes she visualised the kiss as a glass of wine, sweet and smooth and intoxicating. As their mouths explored and tasted each other she gave herself up to the sensation, melting against him, sliding her arms around him, to caress the strong muscles of his back. Suddenly he released her and looked down into her eyes.

'If we're making a new start I may as well make a confession to you. I did shave off my beard because of what you said. It was the bit about my *hiding behind it* that got to me. It was so completely untrue. I've never hidden from anything in my life and I didn't want anyone thinking it. But after I'd done it I was furious with myself for letting you rattle me. That's why I was in such a filthy mood this afternoon.'

She touched his cheek. 'You could always grow it again.'

He caught the hand against his cheek and pressed his lips into its palm. 'Do you want me to?'

She looked at him with wide eyes, shaking her head. 'I don't know. Why should I? I don't really know you, O'Rourke. We don't really know each other.'

'I thought you were going to call me Corin.'

'See what I mean? I don't know you.' She felt oddly detached.

He took her by the shoulders and gave her a little shake. 'Damn it, girl! Do you *want* to know me?'

She considered for a moment. Tonight he seemed different, gentler, less volatile. Seeing him with the Andrettis had made him seem more human somehow. He was certainly a man of many facets. Before she knew what she was saying she heard her voice say: 'Yes. I think I would.'

'Right!' He started the engine and threw the car into gear. A few moments later they were speeding through the busy Friday evening West End traffic. Cara looked at him. His profile was dark and determined and almost immediately her stomach knotted. What had prompted her to reply like that? She must have drunk more of that Italian wine than she realised. How did O'Rourke mean to further their acquaintance? The question rose in her mind, but she didn't dare voice it. Tonight was a night for surprises.

When they stopped outside the mews studio butterflies began to stir Cara's stomach. The practical side of her mind, somewhat submerged by the wine and the relaxed evening behind her, told her that boats were about to be burned, but she pushed the thought aside. The smoke was in her eyes, not in her nostrils, and when O'Rourke held out his hand she put her own into it willingly and followed him up the stairs.

In the living room he switched on a table lamp and took off his jacket, throwing it over the arm of a chair. He slipped a cassette into the stereo and the music of Delius softly permeated every corner of the room. His eyes holding hers, he came slowly to where she stood in the centre of the room and looked down at her. She stared up into the hypnotic blue eyes. Why didn't he touch her—take her in his arms? Her whole body tingled with anticipation. It was like standing on the edge of a swimming pool, wanting to dive in but knowing the water would shock. She looked up at him, her breathing shallow and her lips slightly parted, then, unable to bear the tension any longer, she reached up deliberately and wound her arms around his neck, raising her face to his. When he bent his head she stood on tiptoe and kissed him, gasping when his arms suddenly went round her, almost lifting her feet from the ground and crushing the breath from her body. His lips explored her face passionately, pausing in the hollows of her cheeks, her eyelids and the corners of her mouth; moving to caress her ear with warm breath and tongue, then down to her throat, pausing against the tell-tale throbbing of the pulse there.

'I knew that layer of ice was thin,' he whispered, his warm lips against her ear stirring her senses. 'I knew there'd be fire underneath. Burn for me, Cara—*burn*!'

She knew she didn't have to tell him that she *was* burning—knew he must feel the drumbeat of her heart, just as she could feel his as they clung to each other. She felt him fumbling for the fastenings of her dress, wanting to help him, yet unwilling to appear too eager. Then, the last of her inhibitions gone, she was unbuttoning his shirt, rubbing her face against the roughness of his chest, drawing a groan from him by the movement of her lips and tongue against his skin. As the silky material of the dress slipped to the floor, he swung her effortlessly up into his arms and carried her across the room. On the other side of a small hall he shouldered another door open and she saw that they were in his bedroom.

In the light filtering through from the living room Cara saw their images reflected dimly in the mirrors that lined the opposite wall; watched, fascinated, as he stripped the last of her undergarments from her trembling body then quickly shrugged off his own. Very slowly his gaze moved over her before he reached out for her, drawing her close, enveloping her softness in strong, hard arms as they sank together onto the bed.

His hands tangled in her hair as he kissed every inch of her, making her quiver with delight as his lips and tongue explored her most secret, tender places. His touch inflamed her with a passion and desire she had never dreamed possible.

Gently, he encouraged her to return his caresses, employing supreme control as, hesitantly at first then becoming bolder, she discovered the strong, sensuous delights of his body. Her tumbled hair swept down his body as she rubbed her lips softly against the rough and smooth textures of him; discovered with tender hands the sculpture of his abdomen and thighs. Then, with a sudden cry he seized her shoulders and pulled her up, turning her over and rolling onto her. His open mouth was on hers and she arched towards him, welcoming the weight and mastery of his body, eager for the final culmination of his love. A small involuntary cry escaped her lips as his mouth left hers and he raised his head to look down at her, his eyes suddenly wary. 'Cara!' His voice was ragged and husky. 'Cara—you're not—you're not a virgin, are you?'

She stared up at him, unable to speak, feeling as though the world had suddenly stopped spinning.

His eyes narrowed and he let out his breath in a long, low groan as he rolled away from her. He lay for a moment, his back towards her, then he sat up and began to pull on his clothes.

Suddenly the heady intoxication that was made up of wine and lovemaking ebbed out of her. Rolling herself in the tumbled bedspread she shivered with misery, wondering what sin she had committed to make him so angry. At last he turned to look at her, demanding: 'Why didn't you tell me?'

'I didn't think I had to—did you think I was the type who sleeps around? Is being a virgin a crime? Something—something one has to *confess*?' Tears of humiliation filled her throat and welled up to slide down her cheeks.

He reached across to touch the wetness on her cheek with the tip of one finger and his expression softened. 'Darling, of course it isn't a *crime*,' he said softly. 'It's just . . .' He lifted his shoulders helplessly. 'It's a new experience for me—something I didn't expect—that I've never had to cope with before.' He shook his head and bent to drop a chaste kiss on her forehead. 'I understand so much more about you now. Before, I thought you were cool, completely in control—then—the way you responded . . .' He shook his head. 'But I might have known. You had a lot of wine. I was . . .' He ran an abstracted hand through his hair. 'Oh *Hell*! The more I say the more I'm putting my foot in it!' He touched her cheek. 'Get dressed. I'll make you some coffee, then

I'll take you home.'

She caught his arm, misery filling her heart till it felt like lead. 'No! Don't go, Corin. Why should it make any difference? I don't understand.' She plucked at the sheet miserably, unable to meet his eyes as she whispered: 'You said I'd ask to stay next time. Well, all right—you win. I'm asking. Aren't you pleased?'

He sprang away from her, shaking his head as he looked down at her. 'Don't throw that at me!' he said angrily. 'Do you think I planned this as some kind of *revenge*? Did you really take me for *that* kind of a bastard? No. I couldn't—can't.' He looked down at her, his expression softening. 'Look—I'm sorry. Maybe you were right when you said we were poles apart. You are so different from the girls I'm used to. I'd feel ...' He spread his hands helplessly. 'I don't know—*responsible*, I suppose, and I don't want it to be like that.'

When he had gone she climbed into her clothes and stared at her dim reflection in the mirror hardly able to believe this was actually happening. Could he possibly know how utterly humiliating his actions were, she wondered? Did he really think that being her first lover would have made her some kind of burden to him?

She would have liked to leave at once but he had insisted that she drink the coffee he had made. Reluctantly she gulped it down, scalding her mouth and throat in her eagerness to be gone. Later she sat silently beside him as he drove her home. The beautiful evening that had begun so light-heartedly and gone on to such heights of self-discovery, was over and in ruins.

As she lay awake in her own bed later, the irony of the situation stung her to fresh tears. She hadn't wanted to go out with O'Rourke this evening. If he had left her alone none of this would have happened. Now she knew beyond any doubt that she was in love with him—there was absolutely no use in trying to deny it. But she also knew with equal conviction that all *he* wanted was an attractive, experienced woman with whom he could have an hour's sensual pleasure. A casual fling with no ties.

She rolled over and stuffed her clenched fist into her mouth in an agony of regret. Oh, *why* did he have to insist on taking her out this evening? Why couldn't he have left well alone? If *only* she could wipe out this evening—turn back the clock!

CHAPTER SIX

Cara woke next morning with a splitting headache and was halfway out of bed before she remembered that it was Saturday. She greeted the realisation with mixed feelings.

Normally she would have been relieved to go back to sleep for another hour, but today was different. Today she needed the diversion work would have given her.

With a groan she lay back on the bed, closing her eyes as the finer details of last night's humiliation slowly filtered back into her memory. It was a story O'Rourke would dine out on for weeks, she told herself bitterly. She imagined him telling his smart, sophisticated friends over a drink, 'Who would have thought a girl like that—in this day and age ...?' She shook her head, trying to be fair—telling herself she was doing him an injustice. He had tried to be kind, making her coffee and trying to explain his feelings, even if he did fail to make her understand them. She remembered his gentle, chaste kiss as they had parted. It had felt very final, very like a goodbye—the kind of kiss one would give a disappointed child. He'd said nothing about seeing her again.

'Just as well. It would never have worked,' she told herself aloud, with false bravado, as she rolled out of bed and made her way to the bathroom. 'Never in a million years! I'd never be able to look him in the face again anyway,' she told her reflection in the mirror as she waited for two headache tablets to dissolve in a glass of water. 'He was right about my having had too much wine!' She blushed as she remembered their intimacy in the bedroom of the studio, but even so, her senses stirred at the memory and she turned on the taps and stripped off her nightdress, grateful for the cold rush of the shower to cool her thoughts.

But even though the tablets and the shower helped her hangover, there was nothing she could do about the miserable sinking feeling in the pit of her stomach or the small voice that kept repeating mockingly: *Why did you throw yourself at him like that? How can you be so naive—so stupid as to fall in love with a man like O'Rourke? It would have been obvious to a schoolgirl that all he wanted was a one-night stand.* She clamped her hands over her ears, trying to shut it out. Oh, she was so sick and tired of that small voice!

She picked her way through an early lunch, telling herself it would help to eat something—insisting to herself that she was *not* off her food. After she had washed up she dressed, caught a bus up to The Strand and bought a ticket for the matinée of 'Goodnight Miss Jones.'

As she sat watching Clive she thought she could detect signs of boredom in the way he played his part. Of course, it had been a long run, but it was beginning to be ludicrous, his playing these frothy glamour parts. A pity too, when he was such a good actor and capable of so much more.

She had seen the play twice before and her mind kept wandering as she sat there, slipping back to last night, so that she fought a constant battle with herself, dragging herself again and again back to Clive's problem. She wondered whether or not his agent had been on to him yet about the part in Janet's play. As the third act drew to a close she wondered whether to go round and see him. She still had this argument with herself every time she felt like visiting her father. She was so anxious not to appear to be taking advantage. Horrified at the thought of becoming a nuisance—a bore who always turned up at the wrong moment, or when he wanted to be alone. But as the curtain came down on the last call she made up her mind. If she was to help him—even though he didn't realise it—she must find out what was happening—even at the risk of being thought a nuisance.

She found him in a completely different mood than the last time she had seen him. He seemed younger, more vital and full of energy. The reason soon became clear. The moment Briggs had been despatched to buy cakes he turned to her and took both her hands.

'Darling—guess what?'

She looked into the gleaming blue eyes, some of her lethargy leaving her as she caught his infectious good humour. 'I don't know—something exciting by the look of you. What is it? A film—a new play?'

'Better—a television,' he told her. 'And not only that; it's something completely new for me. An acting challenge—and *more*—a new image.' He turned to look into the mirror, turning his face this way and that. 'How do you fancy me as the mature, world-weary type?'

She smiled, surprised and happy that he had taken to the idea so eagerly. At least she could congratulate herself on that. 'Well, it'll mean acting, but you can do it. I know you can,' she assured him.

Clive turned to hug his daughter. 'Bless you. You always say *exactly* the right thing! You're so good for my ego. I must admit that I had reservations at first, but Max, my agent, took me out to lunch and we had a long talk. He convinced me in the end.'

'Great! I'm glad.'

Over tea she got him to tell her about it.

'It's all rather hush-hush,' he confided. 'That's why even Briggs doesn't know yet.' He smiled at her. 'I know I can trust you not to breathe a word. The thing is, it's by that woman who writes the bestselling romances—Janet Lorimar. But it isn't in the least like anything she's done before. I've already read the script and I'm quite excited about it!' He leaned towards her with an eagerness she hadn't seen in him for some time. 'The character I play is an actor—a playboy type who is losing his grip on everything; over the hill. He's a bit of a stinker, yet there's pathos at the same time.' He smiled happily. 'It really is a superb part. Could launch my career all over again if I pull it off.'

'Of course you will!' Cara breathed a sigh of relief, realising with surprise that Clive hadn't actually identified with the character at all. To him it would all be acting. Max Frazer, his agent, must be more of a diplomat than she had given him credit for!

Clive's face changed as he looked at her. 'But how about you? Here I've been prattling on about my own plans. I haven't even asked you how you are!'

'Me? I'm fine,' she told him.

He looked at her, a small frown creasing his brow. 'I don't think you are. You look peaky.'

She forced a laugh. 'A hangover! I went out to dinner last night and had too much wine. My fault.'

He looked at her for a long moment. 'Poor love. Everyone cries on your shoulder. Who do you go to with *your* troubles?'

She shrugged. 'I don't have any.'

'Truly?' He raised an eyebrow at her enquiringly.

'Truly.'

He took both her hands in his again. 'Listen—I've been thinking—It's time you and I were seen about together. I want to show my lovely girl off. As soon as this load of junk closes—and that could be very soon now—I want us to start going about together. Right?'

Cara's heart lifted. 'Oh, Clive, that would be lovely.'

'That's settled then.'

Briggs came into the dressing room at that moment and began discreetly laying out Clive's costume for Act One. Looking at her watch, Cara realised that it was time for them to start preparing for the evening performance. She got up and began to put on her coat.

'Time I was off.' She kissed Clive and smiled across at Briggs. 'Bye, Briggs. Thanks for the tea.'

'I'll come up to the stage door with you, Miss Dean,' he said. 'I want a word with Bert anyway.'

As they walked along the corridor he grinned at her. 'Did you see a change in him? He's better, isn't he?'

She smiled back. 'Much.'

'He thinks I don't know about this T.V. thing so I play along.'

'You know?' She looked at him. Not much escaped the shrewd little man's notice. He grinned.

'He left the script lying about and he doesn't exactly *whisper* on the telephone when he's excited about something. I could hardly help knowing.' He smiled at her. 'Best thing that's ever happened to him, if you ask me.'

Cara smiled back. At least Clive's life seemed to be back on course. At least she wouldn't have to worry about him any more.

Back in her flat the evening that stretched

108

ahead of Cara seemed endless. She leafed through the paper but there didn't seem to be anything on television. She tried to settle down with a book, but after re-reading the same page three times without taking in one word, she threw it into a corner and got up to make herself a cup of coffee. Looking out of the kitchen window, she saw that it had begun to rain and, as though in sympathy with the raindrops on the pane, tears of self-pity began to slide down her cheeks. Her life was like an English summer, she told herself. Two days of sun, paid for by a week of rain! Why couldn't she be like all the others—taking things lightly at face value—enjoying a casual relationship and then forgetting it? Maybe her background *did* have something to do with it after all. Perhaps there hadn't been enough love and security in her life. She turned from the streaming window, impatiently snatching a sheet of kitchen tissue from the roll and dabbing at her cheeks. Tears would get her nowhere. How *stupid* she must appear. She deserved to be laughed at!

*　　　*　　　*

It rained for the rest of the weekend, but in spite of Monday morning being no brighter, Cara was glad to go back to work. When she walked into Anita's office, however, the older woman looked up at her with concern, pushing her glasses up into her hair and furrowing her brow.

'My God! What on earth have you been doing to yourself?'

To Cara's horror, her lip began to tremble. She tried to turn away before Anita could see, but she couldn't hide her misery from the shrewd eyes.

'Hey! Don't run off like that. Sit down,' Anita commanded. Cara weakly obeyed and the editor flicked the switch of the office intercom. 'Jennifer. Don't put through any calls until I tell you and I don't want to be disturbed for the next ten minutes—right?' She switched off and looked at Cara.

'There! Now—want to tell me what it's all about?'

Cara took a deep breath. 'It's nothing, really. Just Monday morning blues,' she said unconvincingly.

'Looks as though it's been with you all over the weekend!' Anita remarked. She leaned forward. 'Are you feeling off-colour? Would you like to go home and rest?'

'No!' Cara looked at the hands that lay clenched tightly in her lap, horrified at the thought of returning to her lonely flat. 'No— I'd rather be here—working.'

'What is it—a man?' Anita asked gently. When Cara nodded she sighed. 'I thought so. You have all the signs. What's the problem then? Is he married?'

110

'No, nothing like that,' Cara told her quickly. 'It's just that he isn't serious about it and—and . . .'

'You *are*.' The older woman shook her head. 'And to think it was only the other day that I warned you about falling for that type.'

Cara looked at her hopelessly. 'So you see—there's nothing anyone can do about it. I'll just have to work it out of my system.' She made to get up but Anita stopped her.

'Just a minute! Look, Cara, at the risk of appearing nosey, how do you know this guy isn't serious?'

Cara frowned. Every word was like twisting the knife in the wound. Why couldn't Anita leave the subject alone? She couldn't possibly bring herself to tell her the whole story. 'He left me in very little doubt.' She swallowed hard. 'He seemed to see me as the sort of responsibility he could well do without,' she said haltingly.

'Rat!' Anita said succinctly. 'Surely you can see that you're better off without that kind?' She sighed. 'What am I saying?—Of course you can't see it or you wouldn't be so miserable.'

'I feel so foolish—and so angry with myself. To have gone out with him, drunk too much wine and then . . .' She bit her lip. 'To have fallen for an old trick like that—and then taken it for the real thing!'

Anita grinned in spite of her sympathy. 'The

111

classic seduction!' She shook her head. 'I'm afraid it's as old as the world, love. And unfortunately it still works. At least, the first time round. You'll just have to chalk it up to experience and make sure you don't fall for it again.' She reached across the desk and grasped Cara's arm warmly. 'Cheer up, sweetie. No man's worth that much *angst*. I'll get Jennifer to bring us some coffee and we can talk about that feature on the new slimming diet you were going to work on, eh? You were right—work *is* the answer!'

*   *   *

By Wednesday evening the weather had improved and with the help of plenty of hard work and concentration, Cara had managed to get her emotions under control; at least on the surface. In her heart she knew that Anita was right—no man was worth the torture she had put herself through over the weekend. Why, O'Rourke himself had most probably forgotten all about the incident by now—found himself another, more experienced girl who would take life as casually as he did. So why should she worry? At least that was the way she knew she *should* be thinking. The reality was rather different. Inside the shell she had built around it, her heart was still bruised and battered. She still couldn't think of him without her senses reeling—still couldn't trust herself to go through the events of that evening in his studio. Time would heal the wound, her practical small voice told her. But just how *much* time, was what she wanted to know. Was she destined to be an emotional cripple for the rest of her life—just because of a man like O'Rourke?

As she was fumbling in her bag for her key outside her flat, she noticed that the geraniums were coming out in the window box outside the landing window. The sight of the bursting scarlet buds gave her spirits a little lift. Then she heard it. Inside the flat the telephone was ringing. It would be Clive. He had promised to let her know the moment he had signed a contract. She found the key and pushed it into the lock. It stuck and she swore under her breath as she twisted it this way and that. By the time she finally got the door open and reached out her hand to pick up the receiver, the ringing ceased abruptly in mid-ring. Crossly, she threw down her handbag and briefcase. Damn! How frustrating. She looked at her watch. He wouldn't have time to ring her again before curtain up.

She was washing up her supper things when it rang again. This time she was there in an instant.

'Hello. Cara Dean speaking.'

'Cara—hello there. It's Corin O'Rourke. How are you?'

'Oh!' She was taken aback—totally

unprepared for her reaction to the sound of his voice—for the sudden sickening lurch of her stomach. She swallowed hard, groping for a chair and sitting down. 'I'm fine!' She thought her voice sounded false—too high-pitched.

'I'm glad.' There was a pause, then he said: 'I wondered if you were doing anything this evening.'

She stared at the receiver, hardly able to believe her ears. That he could calmly ask her ... 'I—yes, I am, as a matter of fact,' she lied.

'Ah—well, it was rather short notice. What about tomorrow?'

Cara moistened her lips. 'Was it to do with work? I mean, I'll be in the office all day tomorrow.'

'Cara. I want to see *you*.' His voice was urgent. 'I've been thinking about you a lot since—since last week.'

'Have you? I can't think why!' she said crisply. 'Personally I've put the whole thing out of my mind. I think the sooner you do the same, the better!'

He gave an audible sigh. 'Oh dear. It's worse than I thought,' he muttered. 'Cara, just give me a break, that's all. I want to see you—to talk to you.' There was a touch of impatience now in his voice and she felt anger stirring inside her. He really did have a nerve, ringing her up just when she was beginning to feel better, starting things off all over again.

'I'm sorry but I'm tied up all this week,' she told him. 'And even if I weren't, I don't think I'd want to see you, Corin.' Her hand flew to her head. *Corin! Why had she called him Corin?* She bit her lip as he answered wryly:

'At least you only *think* you wouldn't. That's a start. I'll ring you again.' Before she could say another word he had rung off and she was left staring at the buzzing receiver in her hand.

The telephone rang again twice that evening but she didn't answer it. It was unlikely to be Clive and she had told O'Rourke she was going to be out. She had no intention of being caught out. The following evening the phone rang just as she was getting into bed. She picked it up crossly.

'Don't you know it's half-past eleven?' she enquired without waiting to find out who it was.

'As you seem to be out a lot I thought this was the best bet,' he told her calmly. 'You weren't asleep, were you?'

'Yes!'

'Oh—that's too bad. I'm sorry.' He sounded genuinely concerned and for some reason this made her see red. 'Look, if that's all you rang for . . .'

'Don't hang up. It isn't!'

The hand holding the receiver hovered. Should she hang up? Common sense told her to—and yet . . . 'Oh—what do you want?' she

115

snapped. 'Get it over with, will you?'

'Do you like Shakespeare?' he asked.

'Look, is this some kind of joke?' she asked suspiciously. 'Because if it is I don't think it's in the best of . . .'

'It *isn't* a joke. Do you?'

'Well, yes. I do, as a matter of fact,' she admitted grudgingly. 'Why do you want to know?'

'I have to go up to Lincolnshire on Saturday to take some photographs of an open-air performance. I go every year and it's usually an enjoyable evening out. Come with me?'

'Why me?'

'Because I'd like you to. If the answer's yes I'll pick you up at around three. That should give us plenty of time to drive up.'

Cara sank onto the edge of the bed. His voice with its seductive Irish lilt was weakening all her resolve—turning her legs to jelly in the dismayingly familiar way. That maddening small voice urged her: 'Tell him to go to hell! Send him packing once and for all!' She steeled herself to say 'no', took a deep breath and spoke—but somehow the words that came out were—

'Well, all right then.'

Afterwards she sat for a long time, staring at the telephone as she cursed herself for her weakness. Half of her hated the feebleness that had made her agree to something that could well start off another tangle of complications in her life. But that half wasn't strong enough to calm the excited tingle of anticipation in her heart.

Saturday dawned with a fine heat haze dancing over London's rooftops. Cara was up early. She hadn't slept well, partly due to the heat and partly due to the thought of spending a day with O'Rourke. Why in heaven's name had she agreed to go to Lincolnshire with him? How would she face him? What on earth would they find to talk about during the long drive?

She cleaned the flat through thoroughly, glad to have something to do to take her mind off what she thought of by now as the coming ordeal. She ate a salad lunch, then showered. Surveying herself in the bathroom mirror afterwards she was glad of the lunch hours she had spent on the roof of the office block, sunbathing. Her skin glowed golden, giving her a healthy sunkissed look. She chose a dress of fine white cotton splashed with misty, pastel-colours and slipped her bare feet into a pair of strappy white sandals. Scooping her hair into a loose knot in the nape of her neck she took a final look at herself in the mirror and added a touch of her favourite perfume. She was just about to glance at her watch when the urgent buzzing of the doorbell made her jump. Smoothing her skirt and taking a deep breath to try to calm her racing heart, she walked into the hall and opened the door.

He stood on the threshold, a quirky smile on his lips. Before she could speak his hand came out from behind his back handing her a bunch of dark red roses.

'I believe this is the customary gesture of penitence,' he said, looking far from penitent.

She took them from him. 'Thank you—but you really shouldn't have troubled.'

He looked past her into the hall. 'Er—may I come in while you put them in water? My shoes are quite clean and I promise not to put my sticky fingers on the paintwork.'

'Of course.' She ignored his flippancy, turning into the kitchen to fill a vase at the tap before unwrapping the flowers. Her face averted, she bit her lip in anguish. This was going to be even more difficult than she thought.

She turned towards him carrying the vase of roses but when she reached the door he stood in her way. Taking the vase firmly from her and putting it on the worktop he held her shoulders, looking down into her eyes.

'Look, Cara. I'm sure we'd both like to get this bit over. I'm sorry about the other night. I handled it badly.'

She refused to look at him. 'It's all right. I don't want to talk about it. I—I don't know why I agreed to see you today.'

'Please—don't talk like that. As I said, I handled it clumsily—said all the wrong things. There's no reason why we can't be friends—is there?'

'I don't see why you want to waste your time on that kind of relationship. Anyway, I told you before—we have nothing in common ...'

He gave her an impatient little shake. 'Damn it, Cara! You're not making this any easier! What do you want me to do—*grovel*? Do you think it was easy for me to come here like this—cap in hand as it were? If you really want to know, *I'm* as puzzled as you are! When I have all the most beautiful girls in the fashion world at my disposal why am I running after a girl who doesn't even know the score? Perhaps *you'd* like to tell *me*!'

She shrugged his hands from her shoulders with an angry gesture. 'Who *says* I don't know the score? Just because I—because you ...' She threw up her hands in exasperation. 'Oh—I *knew* I was wrong to agree to this. I think it would be best if you left now.'

His hands shot out to grab her as she made to push past him. 'Hell! Here we go again! Okay, so I said the wrong thing again. You should know by now that I'm an expert at it! Just stand *still* and listen to me a minute, will you?' His eyes blazed down at her and she stood still, suddenly sobered as she looked up into them. His voice softened as he went on:

'Right—that's better. Look, Cara, since the other night I haven't been able to get you out of my mind. I kept telling myself what an idiot I was to let you go. I've agonised in case I hurt you. I've called myself ten kinds of fool for saying the things I did. I've argued with myself till I haven't known whether I was coming or going!' He drew her closer. 'The conclusion I finally had to face was that I'm experiencing something for the first time in my life. And I'm sure I don't have to tell you what that is!'

Her lips parted softly as she looked up at him, still hardly daring to believe what he was saying. 'Yes—you do.'

He laughed gently, shaking his head. 'I thought I might, though I've always understood that women have an instinct for this kind of thing. I don't think you have the first clue of the power you have. But the fact that you're not recognising and exploiting it for all it's worth only makes me even more . . .' His arms went round her. 'I'm falling in love with you, Cara.' He whispered, rubbing his lips against her cheek. 'There, I've said it and belicve me, it hasn't been an easy thing for me to come to terms with—or to confess.'

As his lips covered hers she closed her eyes, giving herself up to the heady feeling of surrender. She loved him too. She had been fighting the knowledge all week but now she could give in to it. What was the use of trying to deny it anyway when his arms were so strong—his words and his lips so potent? Wasn't this what she had dreamed of ever since that night?

Afterwards Cara remembered it as a magic

day; a day during which they talked almost non-stop and got to know each other very well. Cara was surprised to find that they had more in common than she would ever have imagined. They liked the same kind of music and the same kind of books. Perhaps best of all, the same kind of things made them both laugh, and laugh they did, their mood light-hearted after the clearing up of their earlier misunderstandings.

On the drive to Lincolnshire the heat haze danced on the road ahead of them all the way and when they arrived at the sixteenth-century manor house in whose grounds the performance was to take place she gasped in delight. It was like stepping back in time. The sun turned the mellow stone of the old house to gold as they drove up the leafy drive and parked in a cleared space. The grounds covered several acres and already the invited audience sat around in groups, picnicking under the ancient trees. Corin opened the boot and hauled out a hamper.

'Our dinner,' he told her briefly.

They spread a cloth on a smooth patch of grass under an oak tree and Cara began to unpack the basket, finding pâté, chicken and salad, strawberries, wrapped coolly in their own leaves, and cream in a special insulated container. There was also a bottle of white wine and a flask of coffee. When she had arranged them on the cloth, she looked at

Corin, her eyes bright.

'It's perfect! But what would you have done with it all if I hadn't come?'

He stretched his long length on the grass, raising an eyebrow at her. 'Eaten it all myself, of course! What else? I'd have needed some consolation, wouldn't I?'

'How did you come to be involved in all this?' Cara asked, looking round as they ate.

'Philip Lock, the producer, is a friend of mine,' he expained. 'He lives in the same village where I have my cottage, about ten miles from here.' Seeing her enquiring look, he went on: 'My little corner of rural England. It's so peaceful—sheer heaven. You must come and see it sometime.'

Before the performance began he went off to take photographs of the players in their costumes. He had explained to her that tonight's performance was a kind of preview, a dress rehearsal for an invited audience consisting of members of the local Shakespeare Society and that he did this for them every year as a special favour, to lend prestige to their worthy efforts.

'Not that they need it,' he added. 'They're already making quite a name for themselves, nationally.'

She smiled at him. 'I thought you never did favours for people?'

'I don't,' he told her. 'At least not for everyone.' The blue eyes looked into hers. 'But you of all people ought to know that there are times when I make exceptions—and I don't *always* have ulterior motives!'

The play was 'Twelfth Night', one of Cara's favourites, and as she packed the used dinner things back into the hamper and stowed it away in the boot of the Bentley, she looked forward to it with eager anticipation.

The performance lived up to her every expectation. The players were excellent and Corin took a good many photographs during the performance for publication in a theatrical magazine. After the show they were invited to have a drink with Philip Lock and his cast.

It was midnight by the time they headed for home. Cara must have fallen asleep on the way, her head on Corin's shoulder and she woke with a start when he drew up and stopped the car.

'Where are we? What's the time?' she mumbled confusedly, rubbing her eyes and looking round. He slipped an arm round her shoulders.

'We're home. You slept most of the way.' He slid a finger under her chin and turned her face towards him, his eyes gently teasing. 'Fine company you are, I must say!' He bent and kissed her softly.

'Sorry,' she murmured. Still unsure of where she was, she peered out of the car window and was surprised to see that they were outside her own flat. Corin got out and came round to her side, opening the door for her. A hand under her elbow he escorted her up the stairs. Outside her flat he looked at her enquiringly.

'Do you have a key?'

She opened her bag and gave it to him. Slipping it into the lock he opened the door and turned to her.

'Well, there you are.' He bent and kissed her surprised face, then, cupping her chin, he kissed her lips, releasing her with a sigh. 'Cara,' he whispered. 'I'm trying very hard to be a gentleman. So will you please get the hell inside and shut the door before my control snaps and I ravish you right here on the landing?'

She wound her arms around his neck and snuggled close to him, rubbing her cheek softly against his. 'What makes you think I *want* you to behave like a gentleman?' she asked teasingly.

With an agonised groan, he disentangled her arms and held her gently but firmly away from him. 'Listen darling,' he said earnestly. 'All my life I've had to grab at the things I've wanted before someone else grabbed them first. Habits like that die hard—and they cloud your judgment. I've never met a girl like you before and this time I want to do things the right way.' Giving her bottom a little slap, he pushed her in through the door.

'So do as you're told, woman. It's four in the morning. Go and get your beauty sleep. I'll ring you in the morning.'

The next moment he was gone, his footsteps echoing down the stairs as she stood there in the doorway, her eyes still sleepy and a little wistful. He had said he was falling in love with her. This time it wasn't a line, she told herself, her heart soaring. He must have meant it! She closed the door slowly and leaned against it.

'Oh, Corin,' she whispered, her heart aching with a sweet tenderness. 'Corin darling, why must you choose a time like this to start behaving like a Jane Austen hero? All I want is the chance to show you how much I love you too!'

CHAPTER SEVEN

She was deeply asleep when the telephone rang. She had been having a muddled dream in which she stood in a garden dressed in Elizabethan costume, watching as two men fought a duel over her. There was a terrifying feel about it, as she seemed to want both of them to win and she screamed helplessly as she watched them lunge at each other thrusting their weapons viciously. Suddenly one of them fell with a cry of pain and she rushed forward, trying to see his face—to find out who he was. But the heavy skirt of her dress hampered her movements and a thick mist hid the men's faces from her view. She opened her mouth to scream—then the telephone woke her.

At first she thought it was the alarm clock and reached out, eyes still closed, to press the button and silence it. But when the ringing continued she opened her eyes and sat up, snatching the phone.

'Hello . . .'

'Darling. I'm sorry to wake you so early.'

At the sound of Corin's voice she sighed and lay back against the pillows, the horror of the dream receding a little. 'I'm glad you did,' she told him gratefully. 'I was having a nightmare.'

He laughed. 'Well! That's nice after spending yesterday with me. You're supposed to have sweet dreams after being with the man you love.'

'Who says I love you, big-head?' she asked him, smiling.

'Do you?' His voice was soft.

'I—I don't think that this is the kind of confession I want to make over the telephone,' she informed him primly. 'So when do I see you?'

He sighed. 'That's just it. There was a message on my answering machine when I got home last night—or rather this morning. From a firm that makes sports-gear. They want me to fly over to Austria to photograph their next season's range of ski-wear. It seems there's a panic on because the snow is melting fast. I have to catch the plane in about an hour from now. I'm sorry, darling. This is a crazy business to work in.'

Disappointment engulfed her. 'Oh—how long will you be away?'

'I don't know. It depends how things go. If the snow isn't good enough we may have to move on somewhere else.'

'But I thought you could rustle up things like that in a studio.'

'It depends on the designer,' he told her. 'This one is a perfectionist. Nothing but authenticity for him. He insists on the real thing.'

'Will you be back in time for Janet's party?'

'I hope so. Anyway, I'll ring you the moment I touch down, okay?'

But after three days of waiting for the telephone to ring Cara decided that he must have moved on to colder climes.

At work she said nothing about her day with Corin. Ever since she had been a very small girl she had had a superstition about the things that meant a lot to her. If you told anyone of your dearest dream it wouldn't come true. And this was one dream that was especially precious to her, more so than any she had ever had.

The party Smithson and Browne's were throwing to launch Janet Lorimar's latest book was to take place on Thursday afternoon at the Westview Hotel in Park Lane. Cara went into the office early and cleared her desk as best she could during the morning. She and Anita ate a hurried lunch in the staff canteen, then went off to change for the party, which was due to start at three. Cara had bought herself a new dress specially for the occasion. It had cost more than she intended but for once she didn't feel guilty, knowing that the look of appreciation in Corin's eyes when he saw her in it would be well worth the cost. It was perfectly plain, but beautifully cut, accentuating the gentle curves of her slim figure; its colour—flame red—setting off her dark colouring dramatically. When she emerged from the cloakroom and Anita saw her she whistled softly.

'Wheew! This is a new Cara Dean! You look quite ravishing in that. Poor Janet won't get a look in.'

Jim Marshall, the art editor, echoed her views: 'Very nice, love; very nice indeed. I wish I got invited to more of these bashes. It isn't every day I get to escort two fantastic looking women like you two!' He moved between them to take an arm of each, grinning delightedly. 'A good job the wife can't see me now!'

Looking back later Cara wondered how she could have set out so light-heartedly. If she'd known what was awaiting her she wouldn't have gone within a hundred miles of the Westview Hotel that sunny Thursday

128

afternoon!

The publishers had taken a whole suite for the party and as Cara and Anita deposited their coats in the sumptuous bedroom that was to serve as a powder room the editor looked at Cara with a wry twist of her lips.

'Nice to see how the other half lives, isn't it?' she remarked.

Cara was enjoying herself, but it was not just the luxury of the sparkling crystal chandeliers or the ankle-deep carpets that had brought a sparkle to her eyes. It was the thought that Corin would be here. True, she hadn't heard from him, but surely he must have returned by now, and knowing the high regard in which he held Janet, she knew he would make it to her launch party if he could, even if it meant coming to the Westview straight from the airport.

Jim joined them in the hallway and they wandered into the large airy room with its fabulous view over Hyde Park. They accepted a glass of champagne from a silver tray carried by an immaculately groomed waiter and moved on to be greeted by Janet, wearing one of her romantic frothy creations—today in elegant black and white. She gave Cara a little hug.

'How nice of you to come—all of you. Do mingle and enjoy yourselves. I'm sure you'll find there are people you know here.'

She was right. As they crossed the room to

where a blow-up of the jacket of Janet's new book plus Corin O'Rourke's newest portrait of her were arranged on a large gilt easel, the crowd parted and Cara caught sight of the back of a head she knew very well. At that moment he turned and his face lighted with pleasure as he hurried towards her.

'Cara—darling!'

Cara felt Anita and Jim's astonished eyes on her as Clive grasped her firmly and kissed her on both cheeks.

'You didn't tell me you were invited to this.' He slipped an arm around her waist. 'Great, isn't it? I was so glad it was on a day when we didn't have a matinée. A lot of very useful people here.' He hugged her close to his side, smiling down at her.

Aware of the curious looks she was getting, Cara cleared her throat and said: 'May I introduce my editor, Anita French? And this is Jim Marshall, our art editor.' She looked at them. 'I expect you know this is Clive Redway.'

Clive turned the full force of his charm onto them as he shook hands. 'Ah—of course. Your magazine is doing a spread on Janet to coincide with her new book coming out. Cara has told me all about it. I'm sure it will be a great success.'

Cara waited, moistening her dry lips. Was he going to tell them he was her father? He did not, instead he drew her away with an apologetic glance at the others. 'I do hope

130

you'll excuse us. I want to have a word with Cara.'

In a quiet corner by the window he heaved a sigh. She noticed for the first time that there were beads of perspiration on his forehead and she asked:

'Is anything the matter?'

He flashed a smile at a couple who were passing, then turned away, his smile replaced by a look of near panic.

'I should say there is. Don't look now but there's a woman standing over there—talking to Gerald Browne. She's an old friend of Janet Lorimar's, apparently. Well, she's . . .'

'An old friend of yours too?' Cara supplied.

He shook his head. 'More of an old enemy!' He shook his head impatiently. 'Oh, we had a *thing*—it was years ago—too damned *many* years ago. Look at her! You wouldn't say she'd exactly worn well, would you?'

Cara looked at him reprovingly. 'You can be so cruel at times, Clive. Anyway, you have a new image now, remember? You don't have to keep your age a secret any longer.'

'But I don't want people thinking I'm ready for the geriatric ward, do I? And if she comes gushing all over me, reminiscing about "just after the war" and all the old wrecks we used to know—in front of all the people I'm here to impress, my chances won't be worth a candle!'

'So what do you want to do?'

'It's more what I want *you* to do, darling.'

131

She stared at him. 'I'm sorry, Clive but if you're asking me to leave with you, I can't. I'm here with my editor and . . .'

He shook his head impatiently. 'No, *no*! I want you to play a part for me—be my girlfriend for the afternoon.'

'Your—*what*?'

'We won't say anything. We won't have to. Just be with me—let them *assume* . . .' He glanced across the room to where the woman was beginning to make her way determinedly in their direction. 'Stay with me as a sort of lucky charm—against *witches*!' He slipped an arm around her waist and gave a loud, theatrical laugh. 'Smile, darling!' he urged out of the corner of his mouth. 'For God's sake look as though you're enjoying yourself.'

Clive's hand was like a vice around her upper arm as they moved among the other guests, but as he went into action she couldn't help but admire the show he put on. As they circulated he oozed charm and appeared smooth and debonair, although she knew by the pressure of his fingers on her arm, the turmoil of his inner feelings.

He introduced her to everyone they met, though he was careful to make no mention of their relationship, leaving his gestures to create their own impression—a possessive little squeeze here—a loving look there. As time went by Cara grew more and more uneasy, especially when, unable to avoid her any longer, they were confronted at last by the woman for whose benefit the show was being put on.

Clare Tremaine had clearly once been very beautiful, and would be still if she hadn't tried so hard to hang onto her youth. Her hair was a rich, too-bright auburn and her face bore the tell-tale taut appearance of recent cosmetic surgery. Wary green eyes flicked over Cara but she addressed herself to Clive, kissing him warmly.

'How lovely to see you again, darling. It's been so long. I've been living in California for the past five years. I saw your show the other evening. So *quaint* that you're still playing juvenile parts. Such a novelty! I admit that I thought you'd have moved on to something more mature by now.'

Clive smiled charmingly at her, ignoring the innuendo. 'And what arc *you* doing these days, Clare? We've missed seeing you in all those lovely *walking-on* parts you always excelled in. Shall you be treating us to more of your talent now that you're back?'

The insult bounced off Clare's diamond-hard shell. Instead she looked pointedly at Cara. 'And who is this pretty child, Clive?' she asked sweetly. 'Your *granddaughter*?'

When they escaped Cara was shaking. Never had she felt so much venom directed at her and she was angry with Clive for subjecting her to it—until she looked at his face. He was sweating again as he reached out to take a drink from a passing waiter. He gulped at it like a man dying of thirst.

'My God, I needed that!'

'I can't think why you let her get to you,' Cara said. 'Why do you care so much what she thinks or says?'

He looked at her impatiently. 'Oh, do grow up, Cara! Look—she's as hard as nails, that one—hard up too. Her marriage fell apart and she didn't get the alimony she hoped for. She's over here on the make.'

Cara shook her head. 'I still don't see . . .'

'I *told* you—we had this thing. I'll come clean. I didn't treat her very well. She's just the sort to sell her story to some bloody rag of a paper, especially if she gets to know about this T.V. play that's in the offing.'

'But if she's a friend of Janet's, surely she *will* get to know.'

'Exactly! Look . . .' He grasped her arm. 'You know Janet. She obviously likes you. Put in a word for me with her, will you?'

Cara stared at him. If only he knew how hard she had worked on getting him the part in Janet's play! 'What kind of word?' she asked. 'Do you want me to tell her the truth?'

'Christ no! If Clare knew you were my daughter God knows *what* she might do!' He looked at her with concern for the first time. 'She might make things hot for you too. No, love. I'm afraid I'm going to have to ask you to

134

sing my praises a bit—plus keeping up the charade we've started this afternoon. I hope you don't mind.'

Cara felt as though she were in a dream as she circulated with Clive amid the popping of flash-bulbs and the buzz of small-talk. He was introduced to Janet's former husband, the T.V. producer who was to put on the play. She felt acutely uncomfortable at the speculative glances that were directed at her and when a distinguished looking man with silver hair came to her rescue and engaged her in conversation she was quite glad to have a diversion for a few minutes.

At about half-past four Clive decided it was time to leave.

'If I don't go now, darling, I shan't have time to relax before the evening performance,' he told her, planting a kiss on her cheek. 'I'll see you soon, I hope—bye!'

She was relieved to see him go and was just looking round for the others when Anita appeared at her side.

'Well! So *that's* the man?' she observed drily.

Cara looked at her. 'What man? *Oh!*' She bit her lip. Obviously, Anita had taken Clive for the man who had been causing her so much agony lately! She opened her mouth to deny it, then closed it again. Perhaps it might be better to let things lie. After all, what could she say? Anita was looking at her with a mixture of pity and disapproval.

'I must say I thought you had more sense,' she whispered urgently. 'Surely you know his reputation? Besides, he may be an attractive, mature man, but he's also old enough to be your *father*!' She glanced at Cara's pink cheeks and added: 'I know it's none of my business, love. I wouldn't mind if he was making you happy, but he clearly isn't. One look at your face right now tells me that!'

At that moment Jim joined them. He gave Anita an apologetic look. 'I don't know if you two are ready to leave,' he said. 'But I have a few things to see to at the office.'

Anita took Cara's arm firmly. 'You're right, Jim. Time we all got back. I'll just find our hostess and say our goodbyes.'

In the taxi on the way back to the office, Cara was silent. If there was one thing she was eminently grateful for, it was that Corin hadn't been able to make the party after all. What he would have made of the afternoon's fiasco, she dared not think!

She avoided Anita when they got back to the office, leaving for home as soon as she had finished her work. As she came out of the underground station she stopped to buy an evening paper. Janet had said that there would be reports of the party in the evening editions.

Slamming the door of the flat she threw down her things and kicked off her shoes. She put the kettle on for a much needed coffee

136

and, while she waited for it to boil, opened the paper. It was on page four. Charles Crane's gossip column featured a full-page report with photographs, Janet's picture and a review of the book taking pride of place. But Cara's heart almost stopped as she stared in disbelieving horror at another picture, given almost as much prominence further down the page. It was of Clive and her. He had his arm around her waist and she was smiling tremulously up at him. It must have been taken at the moment when he had told her to try and look as though she were enjoying herself. Underneath, the caption read: *Hell-raiser's little bit of heaven!* In the top right-hand corner of the article was a small inset picture of Charles Crane, the paper's gossip columnist. It was the distinguished man with the silver hair who had so charmingly engaged her in conversation that afternoon!

CHAPTER EIGHT

For what seemed like hours, Cara sat staring at the words that were rapidly becoming indelibly imprinted on her mind.

It seems that actor and man-about town Clive Redway's amours grow younger and younger. The delicious Cara Dean, an editor for Imperial Magazines, who accompanied him to this

137

afternoon's launch party at the fashionable Westview Hotel, doesn't look a day over twenty and is quite his most delectable conquest yet! If rumour had it—and perish the thought—that Redway was losing his virility, I feel sure that Cara will help him to rediscover it!

She pushed the paper away at last, her stomach churning with nausea. How could the wretched man print such things? How could he have taken so much for granted? Clive had been right when he had said that they would have no need to say anything. But then she had to admit that with his reputation it was hardly surprising! She felt like ringing the paper at once and telling them the truth—asking them to retract the statement in Crane's column. But she couldn't. She was tied hand and foot. She couldn't even ring Clive. He would be waiting for the curtain to go up about now and wouldn't be available.

She stirred herself at last, forcing herself to start making some supper. She had just put the omelette pan on the stove when the telephone rang. She turned off the gas and went to answer it.

'Hello, Cara Dean here,' she said guardedly.

'Cara—it's Janet Lorimar.'

'Oh!' She was surprised. Why was the novelist ringing her? Was she peeved because Charles Crane had given so much space to the photograph of her and Clive? 'Oh—hello. What can I do for you?' she asked hesitantly.

Janet laughed. 'Don't sound so apprehensive, my dear. I'm just ringing to say thank you. I'm flying out to the States first thing in the morning and I didn't want to leave without telling you how much I appreciate your obvious ground-work.'

Cara frowned. She hadn't the vaguest idea what Janet was talking about.

'Ground-work?' she echoed, mystified.

'Now—don't pretend you haven't been working hard on my behalf,' Janet said archly. 'Clive is really enthusiastic about doing the T.V. play and now I understand why. You've been plugging it for me, haven't you? And after all, he doesn't have to worry much about his image when he can be seen with a lovely young girl like you on his arm, does he?' She laughed. 'You really are a dark little horse, I must say! To think that all the time I was talking to Clive's *fiancée*! It almost looks as though I knew and let you see the manuscript of the play on *purpose*. But I can assure you I'd no idea of the relationship between you until today.'

Cara's mouth was dry. She felt like saying 'That makes two of us!' And just where had she got the idea that she was Clive's fiancée, for heaven's sake? Once started this kind of rumour spread and grew like wildfire! With all the control she could muster, she said: 'I really didn't have a lot to do with it. Clive was quite keen to do it.'

'Ah—you can't fool me,' Janet told her. 'Jack—my ex-husband—told me that he had quite a job persuading Clive's agent to offer him the part. Believe me, I know who to give the credit to—and I just wanted to say thank you.'

Cara stared into the telephone, feeling helplessly that the whole thing was getting away from her, gathering momentum like a snowball on a mountain-side. 'Thanks,' she muttered helplessly. 'I hope you have a pleasant and successful trip.'

'Oh, by the way, you haven't seen Corin, have you?'

At the mention of his name Cara felt her knees go weak. 'No—I haven't,' she said, adding silently: 'Thank goodness under the circumstances.'

'Ah—well, never mind. I just thought you might have seen or heard from him during the course of your work, but I guessed he wasn't back or he'd have been at the party. I've been ringing his studio but I couldn't get any reply. If you see him tell him I tried to say goodbye, will you, Cara? Well, better go. I've got to be up at the crack of dawn,' she said brightly. 'I'll look forward to seeing the article you're doing in "Zena" when I get back.'

'I'll make sure you get a copy—'bye.' Cara put down the telephone, her shoulders slumping. It looked very much as though she would have to wait, at least until the rehearsals for the television play were well under way, until the truth about herself and Clive could be released. She only hoped that when the time came she would be able to convince him that the story would help to promote his new image. She was rapidly learning that, with Clive, publicity was the biggest lever!

She watched T.V. and took a long, leisurely bath, trying to soak away some of the tensions that had built up during the day. Midnight saw her making coffee and toast, still too wide awake for bed and when her doorbell suddenly rang, breaking stridently into her thoughts, she started, wondering who could possibly be calling at this time of night.

Going to the door she slipped on the chain and opened it a crack.

'Who is it?' she asked.

'Me—Corin. Let me in, Cara!'

'*Corin!*' Her heart quickening with excitement, she closed the door, quickly slipped off the chain and threw it open again. 'Oh, I'm so glad you're back! I've been . . .' She stopped as one large hand shoved her back against the wall. He pushed past her into the flat and slammed the door shut, his face like thunder as he pushed a copy of the evening paper under her nose.

'A nice welcome back this is!' he shouted. 'God! I can't believe I could have been so naive. To think I actually let you take me in!' He strode into her living room and turned to glare at her as she stood in the doorway.

'Is *this* what you've been two-timing me with?' He took a step towards her, holding out the paper. 'An old ram like Redway? Don't you know that he's had more women than the rest of the acting profession put together?' He shook his head at her. 'You disgust me! You're nothing better than a ...' The word never reached his lips. Cara's hand stopped it with a slap that found its mark like a pistol shot.

They stood, staring at each other, Corin's eyes shocked as his hand went involuntarily to his mouth.

'You little bitch!' he hissed at her through his fingers. 'You double-dealing little bitch!'

Cara was breathing fast. Her inside felt like a quivering jelly; partly from anger and partly from hurt and humiliation. How could he believe that story in the paper without giving her a chance to explain? Simply barge in here after midnight and fling accusations at her without giving her the opportunity to defend herself? Well, if he wanted to believe a story like that, then let him. Quite clearly he couldn't feel anything for her, let alone love.

Although her throat ached with tears and her lip trembled, she thrust out her chin. 'And what gives you the idea you have the right to tell me who to go out with?' she demanded, trying desperately to keep her voice level. 'What right do you have to judge men for the number of girlfriends they have. You're no

142

better yourself!'

Recovered now from the shock of her slap he seized her by the shoulders. His anger filled the atmosphere, almost crackling the air in its intensity. With one sharp push he propelled her into an armchair and towered over her menacingly.

'To think I thought of you as an old-fashioned girl—put you on a pedestal and wanted to woo and win you.' He gave a shout of dry laughter. 'God! What a laugh it must have given you! You really had me fooled, Cara—*me*—the hard-hearted O'Rourke! You *conned* me and that takes a lot of forgetting in my book.'

She stared up at him, shaking her head helplessly, not knowing how to begin to explain; overwhelmed by the hopeless mess she was in. 'It isn't the way it looks ...' she began weakly. He interrupted her with another harsh laugh.

'You're right there! Quite clearly it never has been!' He leaned over the chair, one hand on the back, the other grasping her chin, forcing her to look at him as the blue eyes blazed down blisteringly into hers.

'Listen, I don't give a damn who you go out with or what kind of a stinking name you make for yourself!' he told her, his lip curling in disgust. 'What I *do* object to is being taken for a ride—*and* having your name linked with mine! I don't care to be seen with girls who get themselves plastered all over the gossip columns—girls who'll willingly make themselves cheap just to get noticed and to boost the ego of a has-been like *him*!' He let go her chin and straightened up, hurling the torn and crumpled paper into her lap. 'There you are. There's one for your scrap-book!' He fingered his swollen lip resentfully. 'I may have been stupid enough to shave off my beard for you, but don't think you're going to hang my *scalp* on your belt!' And with this final parting shot, he turned and strode out of the flat, leaving the door swinging on its hinges.

With an effort Cara dragged herself into the hall and slammed it shut, flattening herself against it and closing her eyes tightly. She felt as though all the fight had gone out of her. The anger drained out of her like water from a sieve, leaving her weak and deflated. The tears that had filled her throat with pain erupted in a choking sob, squeezing out from under her closed lids to scald her cheeks. 'Damn you, O'Rourke!' she spluttered, fumbling for a handkerchief. 'Damn you—and damn Clive too!' How could the two men she loved most in the world cause her so much suffering? And how could she be so foolish as to let them?

*　　　*　　　*

She arrived at the office next morning looking hollow-eyed and pale. She was prepared for some kind of repercussion to last night's newspaper article but she wasn't prepared for it to start quite so soon. The moment she got into her office the telephone rang. She picked it up.

'Features.'

'Cara—it's me—Anita. Come into my office, will you?'

Cara's heart sank. She sounded so grave. 'Now?' she asked.

'*Right* now.'

There could be no possible doubt. She was on the carpet!

Anita's face was strained and serious as she looked up from her desk. 'Come in and close the door,' she said. 'Sit down.' She drew a long breath and looked at Cara. 'I don't suppose I have to tell you what it's about, do I?'

'Crane's Column. Me and—and Clive?'

Anita nodded. 'I had the Chairman on the telephone to me at home last night. He was furious. You know what he's like. He hates the name of the Company to be involved in that kind of publicity.' She shook her head impatiently. 'Whatever possessed you to tell Charles Crane you worked for I.M.L.?'

Cara's throat tightened again. 'I didn't know he *was* Charles Crane,' she whispered. 'I didn't know about *any* of it till—till . . .'

Anita shook her head impatiently. 'When you allow yourself to be seen about with someone like Clive Redway you have to be on

145

your guard for that kind of thing!' She sighed. 'What's the situation between you, by the way? I take it he *is* serious now?'

Cara looked up, her eyes opening wide. 'Oh! It's—not what you think,' she began. 'When I told you—Clive and I . . .'

Anita held up her hand. 'Don't! I'd rather not be involved any more than I am already. What I don't know, I can't tell anyone. I've already had the press onto me.'

Cara looked up at her in dismay, her eyes brimming. 'I—take it I'm being asked to resign?' she said in a small voice.

The editor sighed, her exasperated expression softened by pity as she looked at Cara's drooping shoulders. 'I managed to convince the Chairman that I could sort it out. God knows how I thought I was going to do it.' She raised her eyebrows. 'Have you got any ideas?'

Cara shook her head helplessly. 'I told you. It's not what you think. I'd like to explain, but I can't—at least, not yet.'

Anita leaned forward. 'Look. You've got some holiday due. Why don't you take it all at once—now? And for God's sake sort things out before you come back.'

Cara shot her a grateful look. 'Thanks, Anita. I'll work it out—somehow, I promise.'

The editor lifted her shoulders. 'God knows how I'm going to manage without you for a whole month, but it's better than losing you altogether. Try to pull yourself together. You're a damned good features editor. I don't know what got into you—and I don't want to know. Just sort it out, eh?'

'I will,' Cara stood up. 'When would you like me to go—to start my—holiday?'

'I think for your sake, the sooner the better, don't you?' Anita raised one eyebrow. 'Give the whole nine-days' wonder a chance to die down.'

Cara had almost reached the door when Anita said, her voice softer now: 'Cara—look, off the record—take my advice and give him up, love. He'll wreck your life if you're not careful. Ever since this thing started you've looked like nothing on earth! Why don't you go over and spend some time with your mother in Paris? That'd be just the thing for you.' She smiled. 'Why not give her a ring now? Have the call on I.M.L. Anyone asks—I said so.'

Cara turned to look at her, biting her lip, the urge to tell her the truth almost too tempting to resist. But the editor misinterpreted her look of indecision. Shrugging she said: 'Okay, Have it your way. I should know better than to interfere at my age.' As Cara opened the door she added: 'Oh, by the way. Ring Corin O'Rourke for me, will you? Tell him I want his permission to use that portrait of Janet Lorimar for the cover. It was your idea so you might as well have the pleasure of passing the news on to him. There's another matter I want to discuss with him too. It's important, so don't forget, will you?'

Cara's heart sank and she opened her mouth to refuse, then thought better of it. Better not to complicate things still further by trying to explain her reluctance.

Back at her desk Cara slumped, laying her head on folded arms as relief washed over her. It was better than she had dared hope. At least she still had her job. She considered Anita's suggestion. Getting right away seemed a very attractive prospect at the moment and her mother had said in her last letter that they would be pleased to see her any time she cared to fly over. Why not? She reached for her handbag and leafed through her diary for the number, then picked up the telephone and asked for an outside line.

Although they had never been really close, the sound of her mother's voice brought a lump to her throat. 'Mummy . . .' The old childhood name she hadn't used for years slipped out quite naturally. 'It's me—Cara.'

'Cara! Are you all right? Why are you ringing at this time of day? It must be costing you a fortune!' There was a note of alarm in Sarah's voice and Cara did her best to sound reassuring.

'It's all right. I'm at work. My boss is treating me to the call. I've got some holiday

148

due to me and I'd like to come over and see you—if your invitation still holds, that is.'

'Well—of course.' Sarah sounded a little taken aback. 'It would be lovely to see you. Henri will be delighted when I tell him. When would you like to come?'

Cara took a deep breath. 'Would tomorrow be too soon?'

There was a pause, then Sarah said: 'I knew it! Something *is* wrong, isn't it?' Then with great insight she added suspiciously: 'Is it something to do with your father?'

'In a way—yes.' Cara admitted. She heard her mother mutter something uncomplimentary under her breath. 'Look. I can't explain over the phone. Is it all right if I come tomorrow? I can wait a day or two if you'd rather.'

'No, no. Tomorrow will be fine. What time is your flight? We'll meet you at the airport.'

'I don't know, I haven't enquired yet. Don't worry about meeting me,' Cara said. 'I'll come straight there. I've got the address and I can get a taxi.'

As soon as it was arranged she put down the telephone, then picked it up again immediately and set about enquiring whether she could get a seat on a flight for the following day. There was no problem there and fifteen minutes later everything was fixed. She was busy clearing her desk when Jennifer came in with coffee.

'What's all this I hear about you swanning

off to the City of Romance tomorrow then?' she asked with a twinkle.

'Oh—I had the chance to go over and stay with my mother and Anita says she doesn't mind my taking my holiday now instead of later.' Cara crossed her fingers under the desk, hoping Anita's story was similar.

Jennifer confirmed it. 'How boring! That's more or less what the Chief said. I thought you might have met some gorgeous Gallic hunk at the launch party yesterday and he'd swept you off your feet.'

Cara laughed. 'You watch too many T.V. soap operas!'

Jennifer shrugged, then remembered something. 'Oh, I almost forgot. Chief says don't forget to contact O'Rourke before you go, will you? Tell him she wants to see him urgently.'

'All right. I hadn't forgotten.' When Jennifer had gone Cara drank down the hot coffee to fortify herself, then dialled Corin's number, her heart bumping uncomfortably against her ribs. At this time of day he would surely be out, she kept telling herself. She would leave a message on his answering machine. But although she allowed the phone to ring for several minutes she could get no reply at all. She chewed her lip in frustratioan. Damn! He would choose today to go out and forget to switch the wretched thing on!

By twelve she had everything urgent cleared

150

up. She cleared out the drawers of her desk and gathered up her coat and bag. On the way out she tapped on the door of Anita's office.

'I'm leaving now,' she said, looking in. 'I have to catch the bank and get my traveller's cheques. I'd just like to say goodbye—I managed to get on a flight for Paris tomorrow. Thanks again, Anita. I appreciate all you've done.'

Anita looked up over her glasses. 'Just have a good time and remember what I said.' She smiled. 'Oh, by the way—did you get O'Rourke for me?'

Cara shook her head. 'I tried but he was out. He seems to have forgotten to switch on his answering machine too so I wasn't even able to leave a message.'

The editor pulled off her glasses impatiently. 'Blast the man!' She looked apologetically at Cara. 'Look, could you slip round there for me, love? I wouldn't ask but I really do have to see him today. It's for the feature on the new dance studio we're going to do. I've got the go-ahead for him to do the photographs and I don't want to leave it until he's too booked up to fit it in.'

Cara felt trapped. The feature had been her idea so she felt responsible. And after the way Anita had got her off the hook ... 'All right,' she said. 'I'll go round to his studio now. I can always drop a note in if he isn't there.'

Somehow—she didn't know why—she

expected the mews to look different. It was quite a surprise to find the window boxes still ablaze with geraniums and the white-painted doors of the smart little houses as clean and shining as before. In her bag she had an envelope containing a neatly typed note requesting O'Rourke to contact Anita as soon as possible. She had asked Jennifer to do it quickly for her on her way out of the office. Now she stood hesitating in front of the door, the envelope in her hand, wondering what to do. Should she simply push it through the letter box and go on her way? Or should she ring the bell? It might be a chance to see Corin—to try to explain her way out of the horrendous muddle she was in—she would chance it and trust him with Clive's secret. Perhaps his temper would have cooled by now and he would be prepared to listen to her. She wouldn't grovel, she promised herself firmly; quite the opposite. She would enjoy seeing him eat his words—hearing his apology, after which she would tell him she was going to Paris for an indefinite period! That would teach him to jump to conclusions!

Gathering all her courage, she rang the bell. Ten to one he was out, anyway, said her practical small voice—cowardly for once. She waited for several seconds and was just about to turn away when she heard footsteps inside and a moment later, the sounds of the door being opened. Her heart quickened and she got ready to speak the words she had been rehearsing. Then, as the door opened she released the breath she had been holding with a half-gasp.

'Oh!'

The face that regarded her was not O'Rourke's—not male at all, but female and very attractive at that. Cara took a step backwards in confusion to look at the number above the door. Had she somehow rung the wrong bell?

'Can I do anything for you?' the girl asked. Cara looked at her properly. She had opened the door wider now. She was blonde, her hair caught up in a hurried knot on top of her head as though she was about to have a bath. Her feet were bare and she wore a brown towelling robe several sizes too large for her. Cara remembered that robe all too well!

'I—er . . .' Her voice sounded husky and she cleared her throat. 'I was looking for Corin O'Rourke.'

The girl smiled, her delicate eyebrows rising and her delectable pink lips curving like a kitten's. '*Were* you? He's out, I'm afraid.'

'Yes—well . . .' Cara looked down and noticed the note she still held in her hand. She handed it to the girl quickly. 'Would you mind giving him this? It's rather important.'

The girl looked at the envelope for a long moment, then back at Cara with wide blue eyes. Was she just dim or was she being derisive? 'Okay,' she said at last. 'Who shall I say called?'

'I—we worked together on a magazine feature—but it doesn't matter. I mean, the note's not from me.' Cara began to walk backwards, anxious to get away from the girl's mocking eyes.

'But you must have a name,' she called out.

'It doesn't matter. Thank you—goodbye.' She almost ran the rest of the way down the mews, acutely aware of the curious blue stare on her back. It hadn't taken O'Rourke long to find himself consolation, she told herself bitterly.

After the bank there was just one more job to do. It was half-past one when she arrived at the Duke's Theatre and she saw that red printed strips had been pasted up over the playbills outside. They announced: *Final weeks!* So the notice had gone up? Clive would soon be starting rehearsals for Janet's play—if he hadn't already!

The stage doorkeeper wasn't in his cubby-hole and she went straight down to dressing room number one and tapped on the door. Briggs opened it. He seemed surprised to see her.

'Oh—Miss Dean. Mr Redway isn't here yet. He went off to get a haircut.'

'I'll wait if you don't mind, Briggs.' Cara sat down and watched the little man as he methodically laid out Clive's costumes, brushing each garment lovingly, iron at the ready to banish the slightest crease. He seemed slightly uneasy with her today and at last he said: 'Maybe I'm speaking out of turn, Miss. But I don't approve of what he did yesterday and I'd like you to know that.'

She gave him a wry smile. 'Neither do I, Briggs. Thanks for your support. Not that it matters what *we* think.'

He looked up at her. 'Caused you bother, has it?'

She nodded. 'Afraid so. But I'm off on holiday in the morning, so you don't have to worry about me.'

He smiled. 'That's good. Best let the dust settle.' He unplugged the iron and began to fold the board away. 'I suppose you saw the posters outside. The notice is up. Rehearsals for this television thing start next week, so His Lordship's only got one thought in his head.' He looked at her speculatively. 'Have you had any lunch?' She shook her head and he said: 'Right. I'll make you a sandwich and a nice cup of tea. Shouldn't go without in the middle of the day you know. That's what I'm always telling *him*. Not that he takes any notice!' He scuttled away and a few moments later light footsteps outside in the corridor heralded Clive's arrival. When he opened the door and saw her he stopped, the blue eyes slightly guarded.

'Darling! How are . . .'

155

She didn't let him finish. 'I haven't a lot of time, Clive. I'm going away in the morning and I have all my packing to do. I just wanted to say . . .'

He closed the door and crossed the room to grasp both her hands, his eyes repentant. 'Oh darling, *don't*! I saw the piece that swine Crane put in his nasty little column and I can't tell you how sorry I am. I didn't meant it to go further than . . .'

'I think you did, Clive,' she told him coolly. 'I can't tell you the trouble it's caused for me. I just hope it's worth it, that's all.'

He drew his handsome brows together in anguish, but Cara had seen him do it too many times on stage to be impressed. 'What can I *say*?' he implored. 'If there's anything I can do to make up for it, do tell me.' He pushed her gently into a chair and pulled up another, sitting close to her. 'Now—I'm not letting you out of here until you tell me all about it. What's happened?'

She sighed. 'Well—to begin with I've been suspended from my job.' His expression of anguish was sincere this time and she relented a little. 'At least, that's what it amounts to. Officially I'm taking an early holiday. I'm flying over to Paris tomorrow to spend some time with Mummy and Henri.'

His face fell. 'Oh! Well, I expect you'll have a lovely time. By all accounts Henri Labeque is positively loaded!'

156

Cara shot him an indignant look. 'That's the least of my worries!'

'What? What else has happened? Have there been other repercussions? Tell me!' he demanded, pressing her hands.

She shook her head. 'It doesn't matter.' But already tears had filled her eyes. The memory of last night's row with Corin, plus this morning's encounter with the girl at his studio suddenly overtook her and, although she despised herself for letting Clive see her distress she couldn't stop the tears from overflowing. He pulled her into his arms and held her close.

'Oh, my poor baby. What have I done to you?' He held her away from him, looking anxiously into her face. 'Tell me. You obviously have to tell someone and if not your own father, then who?' He fumbled in his pocket and handed her a large pristine handkerchief. At that moment Briggs arrived with the tea and sandwich, quickly assessed the situation and left again discreetly on silent feet. Clive poured a cup of tea and gave it to Cara. 'Here, drink this. It'll make you feel better. Then I think you'd better tell me eveything.'

Cara sipped the tea. 'It's just—well there's someone—a man. I . . .'

'You're in love!' Clive supplied. 'He saw that rubbish in the paper and you had a row!' He threw up his hands dramatically. 'Of

157

course. Why didn't I think of that before I involved you? Oh, if only you'd *confide* in me a little more! If you had, I'd have known!' He looked almost comically contrite. 'Oh, darling! What can I do? There must be something.'

'Nothing,' she said bleakly. 'There's nothing anyone can do. He didn't want to hear my side of it. And anyway I haven't denied it to anyone. I just let them all think it was true so that you wouldn't lose face. That's why I have to go away—till the whole thing dies down.'

He sat back in his chair with a sigh. 'I'd absolutely no idea it would cause all this trouble, honestly. It was just that when I saw Clare . . .' He looked at her. 'The irony of it is that I heard this morning that she flew back to the States this morning.'

She stared at him. 'You mean it was all for *nothing*?'

He hung his head guiltily. 'I feel such a heel! Especially after what you did for me.'

She stared at him. 'What do you mean?'

He couldn't quite meet her eyes. 'I heard that it was you who recommended me for the part. Janet told me yesterday—and even then I didn't tell the truth about us. God! You don't deserve a rotten father like me!' He took her hand. 'Cara. Tell me his name. Let me try to put things straight.'

She shook her head. 'It's too late. It's all over now,' she told him unhappily. 'He's got someone else. I went round to his studio at

158

lunch time and a girl opened the door—in a dressing gown.'

'Studio? He's an artist then?'

'Photographer actually. We'd been working together on a feature.' She shook her head, standing up and gathering together her coat and bag. 'I'm not going to tell you his name, Clive, so it's no use asking.' She bent to kiss his forehead, softening a little at the crestfallen expression on his face. Suddenly she saw how sad and ineffectual he was. He really couldn't see any further than his own reflection in the mirror. For the first time she realised just how unhappy her mother's marriage must have been. 'Look, I've got to go now,' she told him. 'I have a million things to do if I'm to be on that flight tomorrow. I'll send you a postcard with a picture of the Eiffel Tower on it.' She smiled. 'I hope the rehearsals for the T.V. play go well. Goodbye, Clive.'

Outside the stage door the wallflowers in their tubs were dead and no one had bothered to replace them. They seemed to symbolise a turning point—in Cara's life as well as the year. This time tomorrow she would be far away, in France. And when she came back she would have to begin her life all over again. Well, maybe it was all for the best. She turned her footsteps towards Charing Cross, trying to work up some enthusiasm for the trip to Paris, but there was no lift in her heart—no tingle of excitement. All she could see in her mind's eye

159

was Corin's face, twisted with anger and disillusionment at what he saw as her falseness; all she could hear was the echo of his cruel parting words.

CHAPTER NINE

It was nine o'clock when Cara left Heathrow—and raining. Her heart could not have been heavier. But by the time the plane touched down at Orly Airport the sky had cleared and the sun was shining.

Cara passed through the baggage hall and Customs and was making her way towards a queue that looked as though it might be waiting for taxis when a voice spoke at her side.

'Excuse me—would you be Miss Cara Dean?'

She turned to see a man of perhaps twenty-eight or thirty smiling at her. He was of medium height and rather heavily built, dark and typically French looking, though his voice carried only the faintest of accents. She returned his smile.

'That's right—but—er—who . . .'

'Please allow me to introduce myself. I am Jean Paul Labeque. Henri's son,' he explained, offering his hand. 'I have a car. If you will come with me I will take you to our home.'

Somewhat mystified, she allowed him to take her case and followed him out of the building, noticing as she walked behind him, his formal city clothes and immaculately groomed hair. She had, until now, no idea that Henri Labeque, her mother's new husband, had a son!

In the car park Jean Paul stopped and opened the boot of a sleek silver Mercedes roadster, putting her case inside, then he opened the passenger door for her and handed her solicitously in. Cara adjusted the seat belt thoughtfully and when he had seated himself beside her at the wheel, she ventured: 'How did you know which flight I'd be on?'

He shrugged. 'It was simple. I arrived early and met them all.' He smiled at her surprised expression. 'I am on vacation and at leisure so I volunteered. Your mother was concerned; she did not wish you to find your way through Paris alone.' He cast a speculative glance at her, 'She is a little worried about you—afraid you might be ...' He glanced at her apologetically. 'Not quite yourself, shall we say? You are unhappy?' he asked bluntly.

Cara put his abruptness down to the fact that they spoke different languages, but nevertheless, she felt her cheeks redden. 'I'm fine,' she protested. 'I just felt like a change of scene, that's all.'

Jean Paul's dark eyes glinted as he returned them to the road ahead. 'Ah—perhaps an

161

affair of the heart, huh?' Cara made a small, noncommittal noise and he continued. 'You have come to the right place. In France we understand these things better than most.'

Cara maintained her embarrassed silence, hoping they weren't all going to jump to the same conclusion. She watched for a while as Jean Paul skilfully negotiated what seemed to her a complicated traffic system, then asked conversationally: 'Do you live in Paris with my mother and Henri?' Somehow it seemed rude to admit that she hadn't known of his existence.

Jean Paul laughed and shook his head. 'Oh, no. I am a solicitor. I have a practice in Rouen, but I spend most of my vacations with my father.'

'I see. Here, in Paris?'

He shook his head. 'Not always. We have a villa in Nice and we spend several weeks there in the summer. Paris is unbearable when the weather gets hot.'

Cara felt uncomfortable. Had she thrown everyone's plans awry by her unexpected arrival? She remembered her mother's hesitation on the telephone when she had asked if she might come over and suddenly tears gathered, making her throat ache. Why did she have this talent for being in the wrong place at the wrong time? 'I see,' she said slowly. 'I hope I haven't held up your arrangements.'

'Of course not!' he said quickly. 'We were not planning to go yet. And anyway, you would be more than welcome to accompany us.' He looked at her, his eyes sweeping over her with uninhibited appreciation. 'In fact I hope you will. It would certainly make the trip more interesting for me.'

Cara glanced at the handsome profile of the dark and interesting young man beside her. If she had any sense she would go to Nice with the Labeques—enjoy herself with Jean Paul and forget O'Rourke and Clive and the whole messy tangle—if she had any sense!

*   *   *

The Labeques' house was about half an hour's drive from the airport, in a quiet Paris suburb. As Jean Paul drove in through the tall wrought-iron gates, Cara looked up at the white-walled house, its long windows shaded from the sun by louvred shutters. The garden was bordered by tall luxuriant chestnut trees and the delicate filigreed railing of the little balcony above the front door was festooned with ivy and wisteria. She looked up at it as she got out of the car, exclaiming with delight: 'Oh! What a pretty house.'

Jean Paul looked at her with evident surprise, then up at the house which he obviously took for granted. 'Oh? Wait until you see the villa at Nice. It has a wonderful

163

view of the sea. The Mediterranean is so blue at this time of year, isn't it?'

She was just about to tell him she had never actually seen it when her mother appeared at the open front door and came running towards her with a cry of greeting. She looked so chic and elegant that Cara hardly recognised her. It was quite obvious that life in France, married to Henri Labeque, suited her.

'Cara! How lovely to see you. So you found her then?' This to Jean Paul who was carrying her case inside. 'Give that to Pierre. He knows where to put it. Louise has prepared the room at the back overlooking the garden. It's so cool there.' She slipped an arm round Cara's waist and together they walked into the house. It was cool inside; elegantly furnished and carpeted. On the hall table stood a large blue and white Chinese bowl filled with roses in every shade of red. They were reflected in the ornate gilt-framed mirror on the wall which also threw back a reflection of Cara's face as she passed—pale and tired looking.

Sarah led her daughter up the long curving staircase with its wrought-iron balustrade and opened the door of a large, airy bedroom furnished all in white and lilac. On the dressing table were more roses, pale pink this time, their heady perfume pervading the shuttered room. Sarah closed the door and took her daughter's hands, searching her face anxiously.

'You look so tired and peaky, darling. Would you like to lie down and rest?'

Cara laughed and shook her head. 'No, I'll be fine.' She was looking at her mother's sleek new hairstyle and the white dress with its deceptively simple cut. 'I must say you look well. You've lost weight—and your dress! It's so—well—*French!*'

Sarah laughed. 'I'm happy, Cara, *really* happy. Henri is so wonderful. I thought I'd never love another man after your father but now . . .' She broke off. 'But you didn't come to Paris to hear me going on about Henri's virtues. I think you'd better tell me what's been happening, don't you?'

Cara opened her mouth and then closed it again. She had been so angry with Clive, yet she couldn't quite bring herself to put all of the blame on him, especially not to her mother.

Sarah looked at her closely, probing gently: 'You said it had something to do with your father.'

Cara sat down on the bed, feeling suddenly weary. 'It was all a silly mistake really. There's someone—a man . . .' She swallowed and started again. 'Recently I fell in love. After a bad start everything was going well—then there was a stupid mix-up at a party I had to attend. Clive was there and I talked to him. The place was swarming with journalists, naturally. I should have guessed what might happen, I suppose.' She shrugged helplessly. 'In the gossip column of one of the evening papers there was this piece. It seemed I'd been taken for . . .' She broke off, not quite able to say the words. Sarah groaned.

'You needn't go on. I can guess the rest. Of course it was no mistake, Cara. You might as well face the fact that Clive *used* you—latched onto you because you're young and pretty. He isn't seen around with so many nubile young girls nowadays and he wouldn't be able to resist the boost it gave to that flagging ego of his!' Sarah threw up her hands in exasperation. 'Oh! I *told* you to expect trouble if you involved yourself with him!' Her expression softened as she looked at Cara. 'And it messed up your romance? Oh darling, I'm sorry. But why didn't you tell this man the truth?'

'He didn't give me the chance,' Cara told her. 'He was so angry. But there wasn't much I could have said anyway,' she added miserably. 'You see, Clive's never been all that keen on people knowing he has a grown-up daughter— and he had this chance to do a television play and . . .'

She trailed off as Sarah shook her head and sat down beside her on the bed. 'You're much too loyal.' She held up her hand. 'I know— Clive seems to have that effect on people, but he really doesn't deserve it! He obviously hasn't improved with the years!' She took

166

Cara's hand. 'Well, never mind. You're here now. It's done with and we shall have to see what we can do to help you get over it.' She smiled. 'Now tell me—what do you think of Jean Paul?'

Cara shrugged. 'He seems very nice from the little I've seen. It was very good of him to hang around and meet every flight like that.'

'He insisted,' Sarah told her with a smile. 'He's a solicitor, you know. He has a flourishing practice in Rouen and is doing really well. His father worries about him not being married. It's high time he had a wife. It would obviously be a great help to him in his career.' She paused to smile at Cara. 'Life is very pleasant in France. Have you ever thought about leaving England—making a completely fresh start? I can recommend it! It was the best thing I ever did—marrying Henri.'

Cara's heart sank. Her mother was about as subtle as a ton of bricks. Why did everyone seem to think they could use her to fill the gaps in their lives? She was beginning to feel like a door stop! She rose and opened her case, her face turned away so that Sarah should not see how dismayed she was. 'I may not be able to stay long,' she said, feverishly searching her mind for a reason. 'There are lots of people I must try to visit before my summer leave is over,' she added quickly.

'Oh! But won't you come to Nice with us?' Sarah looked disappointed. 'Jean Paul will be there too. We'll all have such a lovely time. You've never really had a chance to get to know Henri. And you've never been to France before, have you?'

Cara turned to smile at her mother. 'No.' She shrugged. Obviously it wasn't going to be as easy to get out of as she thought. 'Well, I'll see.'

The Labeques made her as welcome and comfortable as anyone could, but somehow Cara had to face the fact that her mother now enjoyed a different status. She was no longer merely her mother, she was Madame Henri Labeque and as such, she had taken on a completely new rôle in life. Cara felt almost like an intruder as she sat at the family table and listened to their enthusiastic plans for the summer break. More and more she felt she had no place there in spite of their kindness.

Jean Paul devoted all his time to showing her all the places he insisted she must see whilst in Paris. He was a solicitous and attentive escort and seemed a positive mine of information about each and every one: Notre Dame; le Parc Monceau and the Palace of Versailles; the Louvre and Jeu de Paume; and so many others. After three days her mind whirled dizzily with pictures, gardens, sculpture and grand architecture. Jean Paul made no attempt to hide the fact that he found her attractive. By the second day he was slipping a protective arm around her waist as

168

they walked and although Cara liked her mother's new stepson, she grew increasingly uneasy in his presence. She wished with all her heart that she could have found herself attracted to Jean Paul but it was no use; Corin still occupied her thoughts almost all the time. She had fondly imagined that here in Paris, away from everything she associated with him, she would be able to put him out of her mind, but this was far from the truth. Everywhere they went she imagined she saw him: in the set of a man's head in a crowd; the particular shade of burnished brown hair that was his, glimpsed briefly; a man in Montmartre taking photographs brought a sudden rush of colour to her cheeks. Jean Paul seemed to sense her unease and one day as they were leaning on the white stone balustrade of the Place de la Concorde, watching the ceaseless procession of cars and people, he said suddenly:

'On the day you arrived I asked you if you were unhappy. You said no, but I'm afraid it was not true.' He raised an enquiring eyebrow at her.

Cara shrugged. 'We can't be happy all the time, can we?' she answered evasively.

His hand covered hers as it lay on the balustrade. 'If there is anything I can do to make you happy, Cara, I wish you would tell me.' He lifted her hand to his lips, looking up at her with dark eyes as he kissed the fingers. She felt her heart sink. She had been doing her best to avoid this situation all week.

'I'm afraid there's nothing anyone can do, Jean Paul,' she said, her throat tight with tears. 'I thought that coming here would help me forget.'

He shook his head sadly. 'And now you find it does not work—this running away?'

She shook her head in reply, thinking how nice it would be if she could fall in love with Jean Paul—how perfectly it would fit in with everyone else's plans. Corin didn't love her—he had chosen to despise her without even trying to find out the reason for her actions. He was already consoling himself for her 'fickleness' with someone else, so why couldn't she stop loving and wanting him so much? Her practical mind screamed with impatience at the weakness and foolishness of it all. But it was no use—no use at all. Her heart was still dull and heavy with the painful void he had left in it.

At last she told her mother that she would leave at the end of the week, on the day before they left for Nice. Sarah was disappointed.

'Are you sure, darling? Have you really made up your mind? Isn't there *anything* we can do to change it for you?'

Cara shook her head. 'I've had a lovely time here. You've all made me so welcome, especially Jean Paul . . .'

Sarah looked at her daughter's face and finished the sentence for her: 'But you couldn't

170

feel for him what you felt for this other man?'
She shook her head impatiently. 'You know,
you haven't really given it a chance. I still think
that the atmosphere of Nice—blue sea and
warm sunshine—the relaxed atmosphere . . .'

'No!' Cara said firmly. 'It wouldn't be any
use. I'd only spoil your holiday and I *like* Jean
Paul too much to want to risk hurting him. I'm
sure he understands how I feel.' She twisted
her fingers in her lap, avoiding her mother's
eyes. 'I can't forget *him*, you see. I even think I
see him all the time and it's not going to
improve no matter where I go. I know that
now.'

Sarah sighed. 'Poor darling. I didn't realise
it was quite this bad for you. But believe me, I
do know how you feel.'

Cara looked up in surprise. Her mother had
always seemed to her rather hard-boiled. 'You
do?'

'Of course.' Sarah's eyes softened. 'How do
you think I felt after your father and I split up?
I did love him, you know. Love doesn't
recognise people's faults. Their being weak
and ineffectual—fickle and selfish, has
absolutely nothing to do with their capacity for
making people love them, more's the pity.
Believe me, darling, I know what you're going
through and I promise you it *will* stop
hurting—in time.' She squeezed Cara's hand.
'Look, no need for you to rush off back to
London just because we're leaving. Pierre and

171

Louise will still be here. They'll be glad to have someone to look after. Why not spend a little time exploring by yourself? I think you know your way round fairly well now.'

Cara bit her lip. The thought of going back to London with no work to divert her mind and occupy her was daunting. 'Perhaps I will,' she said at last. 'Just for a day or two anyway.'

Henri had planned a surprise for the last evening they would all spend together. As a special treat he had booked seats for the opera and a table at Maxim's for supper afterwards. Sarah insisted on taking Cara to a chic little boutique she knew and buying her a dress for the occasion. Together they chose a creation in cream chiffon, the skirt a swirl of tiny pleats with a narrow gilt belt to emphasise her slim waist. Gold sandals were bought to complete the outfit, then, the bit firmly between her teeth by now, Sarah hurried her along to her favourite hairdresser to have her hair restyled.

That evening, as she surveyed herself in the bedroom mirror, Cara hardly knew herself. Her shining dark hair shorter, expertly cut in a style that drew attention to her well-shaped head and piquant features, she knew she looked her best. Deep inside she felt a sharp, painful pang. If only Corin could see her. She sighed and turned away from the mirror. No use dreaming of impossibilities.

The four of them enjoyed a wonderful evening together. Cara was enthralled by the opera and later, as they entered the portals of the famed Maxim's she looked around in wonder at the sumptuous furnishings, the great gilt mirrors and the colourful, jewel-like glitter of the Tiffany glass lamps.

Henri ordered champagne and Cara was on her second glass when she looked up. A familiar-sounding laugh, rich and full-throated suddenly alerted her, making her heart miss a beat and draining her cheeks of colour. She sat facing a mirror and, through it, she saw a man who had just come in on the far side of the room. Handsome in his evening dress, tall and broad, his chestnut hair gleaming under the lights—then a crowd of people suddenly stood up, masking him from her view and when they had passed he was gone. Sarah put a hand on Cara's arm.

'Darling! Are you all right? You look as though you've seen a ghost.'

Cara took a sip of her champagne to steady her churning stomach. 'I have,' she whispered. 'The same one I keep *on* seeing—everywhere I go.'

Sarah looked sympathetic. 'I wish you'd change your mind and come to Nice with us, darling. I hate leaving you alone in this state of mind.'

Cara forced herself to smile. 'I'm not in a "state of mind", I promise you. I'm fine— *really!*'

It was almost two a.m. when they arrived

173

back at the Labeque house. Sarah and Henri said their goodnights and went off to bed, but at the foot of the stairs Jean Paul took Cara's arm and drew her into the drawing room. He closed the door and turned to her, his dark eyes grave and admiring.

'You look very beautiful tonight, Cara,' he said. 'I would like you to know that I have enjoyed the days we have spent together very much. I think you are a very lovely and intelligent girl—much too intelligent to waste your time grieving over a dead romance.'

Wary of what was coming next, she smiled nervously. 'Thank you, Jean Paul. I'd like to believe you were right.'

'I am!' he told her firmly. 'Also I think that I could make you forget this man—whoever he is. I have no wish to force you, but if you would let me make love to you ...' As Cara took a step backwards he caught her arms and pulled her roughly to him. 'You must know how I feel,' he said raggedly. 'You must have sensed that I was deeply attracted to you from the moment we met. I think you like me too, don't you—a little at least?'

'Of course I like you,' Cara told him. 'But not ...'

'You have slept with him—this man?' Jean Paul demanded, his arms tightening round her.

Her heart began to beat unevenly. 'I—that's my business,' she told him, her cheeks flaming. 'You've no right to ask ...'

'I thought so! And now he has cast you aside for another love. I would not treat you so.' He clasped her close, burying his face in her neck, his lips against the hollow of her throat and his hands roaming eagerly over her body. His lips close to her ear, he murmured fevered endearments in his own language. Cara was appalled. Surely she hadn't led him to believe that this was what she wanted?

Although she liked Jean Paul as a friend and an escort she found to her dismay that she was repelled by him at close quarters. His breath against her cheek carried traces of French cigarettes and the rich, spicy food he had eaten. The scent of his aftershave was cloying and slightly effeminate to her nostrils and his hands were soft and slightly damp. However much she tried she knew she could never possibly make herself respond to him as a lover. His lips took hers with a sudden passionate urgency, forcing her lips apart, his tongue exploring her mouth while his fingers searched feverishly for the fastening of her dress. With a cry of protest she pushed him forcibly away.

'No, Jean Paul!' she gasped breathlessly. 'Please let me go. It's no use. I can't. I never could. I'm sorry if I gave you the impression that I ...' She trailed off miserably, acutely embarrassed. For a moment she thought he was going to lose his temper. A muscle at the corner of his mouth twitched and the dark

Latin eyes glinted with frustration and wounded pride. Then his good breeding prevailed and he regained his control, smiling coolly and lifting his shoulders.

'As you wish. I still say that I could have made you mine in one night, Cara. I am a very skilled lover.'

She shook her head, rigid with discomfort, longing to get away to her own room. 'I—I'm sure you are.'

He touched her arm. 'Why not, *chérie*? It would be a pleasant way to seal our friendship if nothing else—a very appropriate way to end our short time together. It would surely bring nothing but pleasure to both of us.'

But Cara was already at the door, her hand on the handle. She turned to him. 'You have been very kind, Jean Paul. You've given up a lot of your time to me and I'm grateful—but I . . .'

He spread his hands, shrugging philosophically and giving her a smile that told her plainly that she didn't know what she was missing. 'Ah well—*c'est la vie*. My opinion—for what it is worth—is that both you and this man you have quarrelled with must be quite mad!'

The following morning Cara pleaded a headache and remained in bed. Louise, the middle-aged housekeeper, brought her breakfast to her in her room and she was just finishing it when her mother came in, dressed for the journey. She looked anxious.

176

'You're sure you're all right, darling?' she asked.

Cara assured her that she was. 'I'm fine. I may as well tell you the truth. I didn't come down to breakfast because I couldn't face Jean Paul again. I'm afraid I must have somehow given him the wrong impression last night. It was rather embarrassing.'

Sarah laughed. 'You mean he made a pass? Well what would you expect of a normal, red-blooded young Frenchman? He would have considered it an insult to you not to have done! Believe me, he won't bear you any grudges. I'm only sorry you couldn't have teamed up—if only for the holiday. I still think it would have done you the world of good.' She bent to kiss her daughter. 'Now, remember what I told you. Stay here as long as you like. Keep in touch and if you *should* change your mind you can always come down and join us. Here's the address.' She opened her bag and put a piece of paper on the dressing table. Turning, she gave Cara a last regretful look. 'Well, this is goodbye, darling.'

'Goodbye. Thank you for a lovely time—for the dress and everything. Say goodbye and thank you to Henri too, for last night. Have a super time in Nice and don't worry about me,' Cara told her. 'I'm looking forward to getting back to work. And I've really enjoyed staying here with you.'

She lay in bed, listening to the sounds of

177

their departure. She heard Pierre and Louise calling their cheerful *adieux* and the sound of the car as it gradually receded into the distance. For a while she lay there. The house was so quiet now that they had gone. Just for one wild, panicky moment she wished she had gone with them—wished she had tried a little harder to fall in love with Jean Paul. Was he really so confident that he had the power to 'make her his', as he had put it, she wondered idly? Finally she threw back the bedclothes and swung her feet determinedly to the floor. This wouldn't do. She would shower, dress and go into Paris to explore by herself. It would be an adventure. She told herself bravely that she was looking forward to it—and wished she could believe that it was true.

CHAPTER TEN

Determined to throw off her mood of depression and make the most of what was left of her stay in Paris, Cara decided to visit the Left Bank. Although Jean Paul had taken her to most of the conventional tourist places the time had been limited. But for Cara, *La Rive Gauche* epitomised all the romantic dreams she had ever cherished of Paris and she knew she would always regret it if she went home to London without seeing for herself if it was all true.

Suitably dressed in jeans and a cotton shirt and equipped with a guide book, she set off, ticking off in her mind all the places she must be sure to see; the Old Royal Palace; the Place St. Michel and, at the bottom end, the Fontaine St. Michel, where all the Sorbonne students were reputed to gather.

She was not disappointed. It was all there, just as she had pictured it. But later in the morning, as she sat drinking hot dark coffee at one of the little pavement tables of the *Café des Deux Magots* in the Boulevard St. Germain, she reflected that none of it had lifted her heart as she had hoped. Somewhere she had read that if you sat here for long enough you would see the whole world go by. But in spite of the bustling noise and the throng of cosmopolitan humanity she felt suddenly isolated. All around her people seemed to be in couples, from the chic middle-aged couple chatting quietly at the next table, to the teenage boy and girl so obviously and flamboyantly in the throes of first love, stopping every few yards to kiss as they walked past. As she watched them wistfully from her table the dull yearning in her heart twisted painfully. Paris was the last place on earth in which to be alone.

Looking at her watch, she was surprised to find that it was almost lunch time. Should she stop and eat here, she wondered? Or should

179

she go on with her exploring? There was still so much she must see, she told herself brightly, in a brave attempt to shake off the aching loneliness. It would be terrible to go back to London without seeing the rue St. Severin with its mediaeval lanes, and the Luxembourg Gardens which alone would probably take a whole afternoon to explore.

But the sun was warm on her back as she sat there on her little cane chair and she ordered another coffee, putting off the moment when she would have to get up and walk on alone. There was no need to decide for a moment; no one hurried in Paris.

The waiter put the cup down on the table before her and she glanced up to thank him. Suddenly she was aware that she was being watched. Out of the corner of her eye she glimpsed a man sitting reading a newspaper at a table some distance away. He wore dark glasses and he was unshaven but in spite of the fact that his eyes were hidden she was certain that he was watching her over the top of his paper. She turned her chair slightly and sipped her coffee, trying to appear unconcerned as all the stories she had heard suddenly crowded into her mind. It was said to be unwise for a girl to wander through the Left Bank streets on her own. It was supposed to invite speculation and perhaps unwanted invitations. She drew herself up sharply. How ridiculous in this day and age! She was perfectly capable of looking after herself. Anyway, if she kept to the crowded streets what harm could possibly come to her?

She drained her cup and stood up, glancing behind her as she slipped the strap of her bag over her shoulder. He was still there, though he had now retreated behind his newspaper. Perhaps it was her imagination, she told herself. But all the same, she avoided turning to look straight at him. She consulted her guide-book briefly, then began to walk away, along the boulevard towards the rue St. Severin. Today she would be what Jean Paul had called a *flâneur*—an idle wanderer. The idea pleased her.

She had been walking for about ten minutes when she felt it again—this time it was undeniable, that feeling of eyes on her back— of being watched- *-followed*. She was now in the maze of narrow, cobbled alleys in what the guide book described as the very oldest part of Paris. Here the mediaeval atmosphere still clung to the ancient walls and her vivid imagination soared on lurid wings. Her heart began to race in mounting unease and she quickened her steps. Suddenly a heavily accented voice called:

''Allo! Mademoiselle! You need a guide? I can show you many interesting things—very cheaply.'

Without looking round she hurried on, but the footsteps behind her matched her own pace. Suddenly the alley seemed to empty. Just she and the stranger. Cara's heart bumped wildly against her ribs as she broke into a run, but she turned her ankle painfully on the uneven cobbles and stumbled. A large, strong hand caught her arm and held her firmly. With her mouth open ready to scream she looked up at the face above her. She had been right—it *was* the man from the café—the same one who had followed her and called out his offer to guide her. But as she stared at him he removed the dark glasses, slipping them into the breast pocket of his shirt.

'Don't be scared. It's only me.'

Her eyes widened. *'O'Rourke!'* Anger replaced her terror and she lashed out at him: 'You frightened me half to death! What on *earth* do you think you're doing?' Her inside churned with mingled emotions; anger, relief, shock—and something else that for the moment she refused to acknowledge.

He smiled triumphantly down at her. 'So—we meet at last! I thought I'd never get a chance to speak to you. Where's Fido today?'

She frowned. 'Who?'

'Your watchdog—the immaculate Frenchman you've had in tow all week.'

'That's none of your business,' she told him shakily. Her heart was jumping about so painfully in her chest that for one panicky moment she was afraid she might faint and make a fool of herself. Confusion made her voice sharp as she asked him: 'What *are* you doing here, anyway? Why are you disguised like that? And what's the idea—calling out to me in that ridiculous accent?'

The blue eyes flashed. 'What the hell do you *think* I'm doing! I'm following you! I had to attract your attention somehow, didn't I? And I had the distinct impression that if you'd known it was me you wouldn't have spoken to me.' He rubbed his chin. 'And for your information, I am *not* disguised. I'm growing my beard again! Shaving it off was a mistake.' He took her arm again. 'Let's go somewhere quiet. We have a lot of talking to do.'

She stared up at him incredulously. 'What makes you think I'm going to talk to you—let alone go anywhere with you?' she asked defiantly. Seeing him here like this was such a shock she still couldn't quite believe it was happening. Suddenly she thought of all those other times she had imagined she saw him. Perhaps it hadn't been her imagination after all! Perhaps she really *had* seen him.

He shook her arm. 'Cara! Don't play games with me. Let's find somewhere quiet.'

Suddenly she was furious with him. Did he really think he could calmly walk back into her life after putting her through such misery and expect her to sit down and talk as though nothing had happened? 'I think you've got one hell of a nerve!' she told him warmly. 'Following me all over Paris—dogging my footsteps and firing questions at me. The last time we met you were calling me all the nastiest things you could lay your tongue to!' But the last few words were delivered rather breathlessly because he was propelling her along the street at a smart pace, his hand gripping her arm too tightly for her to escape.

'Let me *go*!' she demanded indignantly, trying in vain to shake her arm free. 'You're hurting me. If you think *this* is the way to get me to listen to what you have to s . . . oh!'

He had stopped suddenly, causing her to bump into him. He turned to look down at her, his eyes blazing. 'Just stop it, will you?' he demanded. 'At least wait till we've had a talk. Then you can have your say. All I'm asking is that you listen. Just give me a break, will you?'

Looking up at him, her throat suddenly constricted and tears blurred her vision. 'Like the break you gave me!' she accused, her voice husky.

He ran a hand through his hair. 'Okay, okay. I know—and you can pay me back later if you still feel like it. Just hear me out first, that's all I ask.' He looked down at her, one eyebrow raised in the familiar way that twisted her heart.

She looked into the blue eyes and was lost. After all she had gone through there was no way she could walk away without hearing his explanation—however incredible it might turn out to be. The overwhelming joy deep in her

184

heart at seeing him again was undeniable, melting away her anger like ice in a heatwave. 'All right then,' she heard herself say.

His grip on her arm relaxed and he picked up her hand, pulling it firmly through his arm as though he still wasn't taking the chance of her running away. 'Right. Had lunch?' She shook her head. 'First things first, then,' he told her. 'Food! And I know just the place.'

She might have known it would be Italian. He grinned at her as they took their seats at the little table with its red chequered cloth.

'The nearest thing I could get to the Andrettis',' he told her—and then surprised the waiter by ordering in his fluent Italian complete with Milanese accent. When the little man had gone, his face wreathed in smiles, Corin looked at her. 'How is it that you're alone today?'

She looked at him accusingly. 'I might ask the same of you!' He looked genuinely puzzled as she went on: 'Before I left London last week I went to your studio. Anita asked me to get in touch with you and I couldn't reach you on the telephone.' She looked him straight in the eyes. 'When I got there a girl came to the door. A blonde girl—wearing your bathrobe.'

He raised an eyebrow. 'Ah—I see. And you put two and two together?'

She shrugged. 'I don't need hitting over the head with a sledgehammer before I get the

185

message.'

His brow cleared. 'So it was *you* who brought that note! I wondered . . .' He looked at her. 'The girl you saw was Zoe Markham, a model I've worked with quite a lot. She rang me that morning just as I was leaving for work. She'd just flown in from a modelling assignment in Bermuda and found that her flatmate had had the locks changed for some reason or other. She couldn't get in till her friend got home from work and she was dead on her feet. She asked me if she could use the flat for the day—have a bath and get some sleep.' He spread his hands. 'You don't *have* to believe it, of course, but it does happen to be the truth. As a matter of fact I didn't even *see* her. I left the key with a neighbour for her and by the time I got home that evening, she'd left. All I found was a brief thank-you note from her—and the other one telling me to get in touch with Anita French.'

Cara bit her lip. 'Oh—I see.'

'Do you?' He leaned forward. 'Anyway, it didn't take you long to find an escort to show you the sights of Paris, did it?'

'As it happens, he was my mother's new stepson,' she told him. 'I've been staying with my mother and her husband. They left for a holiday in Nice this morning.' She glanced up at him. 'Jean Paul went with them.'

'Ah.'

'He was very kind and—and attentive,' she

186

told him defensively.

'Oh, I could see that. He never left you alone for a minute. I've never spent such an energetic and furtive few days. I was beginning to feel like Inspector Clouseau! Last night at Maxim's looked like a celebration to me. I decided to throw in the towel and go back to London. Today was to be my last day. I could hardly believe it when I looked up from my paper and saw you sitting there at the café.' His eyes challenged hers and for a moment they held each other's gaze. Cara was the first to break the silence:

'You still haven't told me why you're here.' She said, moistening her dry lips.

'Surely it's obvious! I came to find you.'

She looked up at him, her eyes flashing. 'You know what I mean. Don't play games with me, O'Rourke. I can still get up and walk out of here, you know.' His hand shot out and covered hers, holding it tightly.

'Don't do that, Cara. I promise you I'm not playing games.'

Their pasta arrived, fragrant with herbs and succulent with a meaty tomato sauce, but suddenly neither of them had any appetite for it.

When the waiter had gone Cara asked: 'I don't understand. How did you know I was here?' She looked up at him. 'And what made you want to find me after that piece in Crane's Column?'

187

'You're not the only one who jumps to conclusions,' he interrupted. 'Someone took it upon himself to put me wise. Not that I deserved it.'

She looked at him, startled. 'Who told you—and *what*?'

His eyes twinkled. 'Shall we say that a certain *bank manager* got in touch with me?' He had her full attention now. She stared at him, her eyes wide. He went on: 'A bank manager you said you'd lost touch with.' He laughed at her crestfallen expression and reached for her hand again. 'Darling, surely you haven't forgotten the great big fib you told me? Can you imagine how surprised I was when Clive Redway telephoned me and asked me to meet him for lunch? I almost told him what he could do with his lunch—until he told me he was your father!'

'*Clive telephoned you?* And—and said *that*?' Cara could scarcely believe what she was hearing.

'He certainly did. He gave me a superb slap-up lunch at the "Garrick" too.' He smiled reminiscently. 'Though to begin with we were at cross purposes. He thought *I'd* done wrong by you and I thought *he* had. The unravelling took quite a long time, but we finished up the best of friends.'

'And Clive told you I was here in Paris?' she concluded.

'Yes, but he didn't know the address.' He

gave her a wry, lop-sided grin. 'I wonder if you realise how many Labeques there are in the phone book? I told you it was a Pink Panther job!' He leaned across the table, his face suddenly grave. 'Why didn't you tell me the truth in the first place, Cara? Didn't you trust me enough? I thought I knew you after the day we went to Lincolnshire together. To me you were so different, so *special*. That afternoon on the plane coming home I was so impatient—so happy and excited at the thought of seeing you. Can you imagine how I felt when I bought a paper at the airport and read that story about you and Redway? It gave the lie to every single line of my image of you! I've never felt so cheated—so shattered!'

She shook her head. 'Why couldn't you have trusted me enough to listen to my explanation? You didn't give me a chance.'

He took her hand. 'I was too angry—too hurt. I felt so let down. I'd never been in love before, Cara; never allowed any other woman to get that close to me—and I'd been conned, made a laughing stock. Or that's the way it seemed to me at that moment.' He gave her a wry grin. 'Does it surprise you to know that you don't have an exclusive claim to feeling insecure? But your father put me straight on what happened and I'm here to make amends—to ask for your forgiveness if you like.' He looked enquiringly at her, his head on one side. 'Well—do I get it?'

189

'Of course,' she whispered, reaching for his hand and twining her fingers in his.

Their eyes locked for a moment, then he looked impatiently at her barely touched plate. 'Look, if you don't want any more of that let's get out of here. I want to take you somewhere where I can kiss you.'

He explained as they walked that he was staying in the studio flat of a photographer friend who was away in America. It was on the Left Bank, only ten minutes' walk away from the restaurant and to reach it they walked through a courtyard shaded by a gnarled old mulberry tree. A flight of stone steps with a wrought-iron railing led up to a small balcony. Corin produced a key and unlocked the half-glazed door, standing aside to let her go in first. She looked around the shabby room that was really no more than a large bed-sitter, smiling at the characteristic clutter, so typical of its present occupant. She turned to comment on it, but before the words could reach her lips she was in his arms. His kiss made her reel, stopping the breath in her throat and whipping her senses to instant desire. His lips on hers were like a match held to tinder. They were hard and hungry, telling her more than words could ever say about the depth of his feelings for her. His arms crushed her close so that she could feel the wild beating of his heart, echoing her own; feel the strength of his body and the hardness against her thigh that spoke volumes of his need for her.

When at last his lips left hers she drew a long shuddering sigh. 'I've been so miserable without you,' she whispered. 'I didn't mean to lie. I couldn't tell you a secret that wasn't mine to tell . . .' He laid his fingers gently against her lips, stopping her words.

'No more. It's all past now. I love you, Cara, and I'm not going to let you go again.' He looked deep into her eyes. 'Say you love me too.'

She shook her head. 'You know I do.'

'You've never said it. Cara. Say it now!' he demanded.

'I love you, Corin.'

He kissed her again, till her head swam, then stood with his arms wrapped tightly round her, his chin resting on her head. His voice was husky as he said: 'If you only knew how murderous I felt, watching you with—what's his name?—Jean Paul. I kept wondering what was going on—thinking of what I'd thrown away. Torturing myself with the thought that you might fall for him before I could get you back. I told you once that I'd always had to grab the things I wanted from life before someone else got them. I can't tell you how many kinds of fool I've called myself for not grabbing you when I had the chance!' He pulled her closer, sliding his hand down her spine to press her to him. 'It was all I could do not to punch him on the nose and make off with you like the pirate you once called me.' He looked down at her, his eyes burning. 'Cara—will you marry me?'

The words sent shock waves through her and she looked up at him for a long moment, her eyes starry, hardly daring to breathe for fear of breaking the spell that hovered over them. 'Are you sure you wouldn't feel—too *responsible*!' she asked softly at last.

He winced. 'What a *crazy* thing to say. How do I ever live it down?'

She stood on tiptoe and wound her arms around his neck, her eyes straying to the tumbled bed. 'There *is* a way,' she whispered. 'Surely I don't have to tell a man like O'Rourke what it is.'

*　　*　　*

The tiny stone cottage dreamed in the misty light of dawn. The first pale spears of sunlight found a chink in the curtains and played on Cara's eyelids, waking her out of a deep, contented sleep. She turned her head on the pillow to look at the face of the man beside her. In sleep he looked much younger, almost boyish and she smiled drowsily, her heart contracting with love as she reached out to touch his hair. Thick, dark lashes fanned on his cheeks and the strong planes of his face were somehow softened in repose. His beard had grown again, a neater, modified version of the wild affair he had had when she first met him. This time he had informed her firmly that it was here to stay—whether it made him look like a pirate or not!

Slipping out of bed, she drew the curtain back and stood at the window. Below, the garden sparkled with dew; a tumble of flowers, both wild and cultivated, growing in wild profusion. Beyond, the Lincolnshire wolds rolled gently away into the distance, veiled in a light mist that promised another warm day. But now the air was fresh and cool, caressing her softly as she stood at the open window. London and Paris seemed so far away.

So much had happened in the past few weeks. Her hurried wedding to Corin had taken place in a registrar's office with a special licence. It had shaken everyone, not least herself, with its whirlwind haste, but as he said: 'I've almost blown it once and I'm not pushing my luck again. This time I'm making good and sure of you!'

It seemed incredible to her that it was barely a month ago that he had said those words. Breathing the fresh, brand new morning air, she tried to remember a time when she hadn't loved Corin and found it impossible. That time was like a half forgotten dream, dreamed by a stranger.

They had decided to come here to the cottage for their brief honeymoon and Cara had never been so blissfully happy in her life. The days had been spent walking hand in hand over the fields and along the leafy lanes as he showed her the quiet countryside he loved; their nights, making love in the big bed that almost filled the tiny, low-ceilinged room; each of them learning so much about the other, falling a little more in love as each precious hour passed. Two more days and their honeymoon would be over. They would return to London to pick up the threads of their working life again. It looked as though there would be a good many claims on their free time. Clive had invited them to a party to celebrate the completion of the recording of Janet Lorimar's play. He was still glowing with satisfaction at the first unselfish thing he had done in his life, and his cleverness at discovering Corin's identity. But Cara smiled as she remembered his ill-concealed triumph at the way Charles Crane had been made to eat his words publicly. The gossip columnist had had to promise not only to retract the scurrilous remarks he had made about him and Cara but also to give special attention to Clive's new image as a serious actor.

Janet herself had heard the news of their marriage and had writen Cara a long letter, apologising for jumping to the wrong conclusion about her relationship with Clive. She had promised to get in touch the moment she returned from the States and to give them a party. Anita too had been shocked to find she had done Cara an injustice, but she was annoyed too, feeling that she should have been let in on the secret. Cara sighed. It would be some time before all the feathers ruffled by the affair were smoothed.

Standing there at the window, she sighed, her happiness tinged with sadness. Although she knew nothing could spoil the joy of being married to Corin, she couldn't help wishing that this magic time alone together could have gone on for longer.

'What is it, darling? Did something wake you?' Corin's voice was sleepy as his two strong arms crept round her. Cupping her breasts he drew her back against him. She turned her head to look up at him.

'Just happiness,' she told him. 'And a little sadness too—that all this will soon be over. I was just trying to remember how I felt before we met. I think I was only half alive. I don't want to go back to London—to being apart from you.'

He bent and kissed her bare shoulder, turning her to him as he felt the ripple of her response. His voice was muffled as he buried his face in her hair. 'We can come back to the cottage any time we like,' he promised. 'And surely you know that we can never really be apart again?' He held her away from him and looked down at her, his blue eyes teasing gently. 'You must know with all your knowledge of them, that pirates never give up their plunder.' He laughed gently, drawing her back with him onto the bed and pulling her close. 'After winning their treasures the hard way they make sure they enjoy them to the full!'

Cara closed her eyes, snuggling up to him in the huge feather bed. You could get a lot of loving into two days—and even more into a lifetime!